Parracombe Prize 2020

short story competition

This anthology has been selected from entries to the Parracombe Prize 2020 short story competition and it is dedicated to all the authors who entered.

ISBN 978-1-8384822-0-6

Published by Parracombe Community Trust

Results of the Parracombe Prize 2020

First prize went to **Anil Classen** for his story **Sento**.

What the judges said:

'The exploration of how a small memory from the past and . the kindness of a stranger can change a life was mesmerising even in a fourth reading. Delicate writing.'

'An incredibly moving story that speaks about tradition, duty and loss. Beautifully written.'

'An elegantly drawn study of the process of grief that sidesteps mawkish sentimentality in favour of core emotion.'

In second place **Emily Howes** for her entry **Little Hell.**

What the judges said:

'Against the grimy backdrop of a poor iron ore mining and smelting community, this story captures shame and disillusionment. I felt each movement and nuance.'

'The abandonment of a Welsh community marginalised to a slag heap during the Industrial Revolution underlines this awkward, jarring encounter. The weight of disappointment set against the certainty of a bleak and hopeless future emanates from every line.'

'A starkly painted portrait of utter despair, which poses the question as to whether you should ever leave and if you can ever return.'

Jointly in third place was **Ali Said** with **Both at Once** and **Conor Duggan** with **The Egg and the Skipping Rope**.

A further 31 stories were long-listed.

Contents

Sento

Spring was the hardest season for Akira. It may have been the season of blossoms as Tokyo exploded into clouds of pink paper fireworks, the colour of candyfloss, but every single flower seemed to tug at him. He tried not to notice the hordes of people gathering on picnic blankets for that time of year when the city was masked, the grey cement and roar of commerce momentarily overshadowed by a sense of frivolous hope. All of it made him angry, the eyes of young mothers lighting up with delight as their babies looked up at the trees overhead, the perfect moment to snap that perfect photograph, one of too many already posted online, another one for the archive that did not interest anyone.

After he stowed his clothing in the perforated locker that allowed everyone a peek inside, he tied a tiny white towel around his waist and walked towards the glass sliding door that led to the washroom. This was his ritual, the one his father had established, the one his classmates had ridiculed. His home did not have the bathroom so many other children took for granted. Akira hated his parents for their poverty. He wanted to blend in. Back then, sticking out was not something to strive for. It was easier being part of the pack even if it was a pack of dogs. When he started making his own money, he could not stop himself from returning to the bath house. This was more than just a place to bathe. Everything here seemed to whisper to him in soft tones. The oversized depiction of Mount Fuji loomed over three deep pools where men sat with their towels folded in rough squares on their heads as they spoke quietly with each other. The sound of water permanently running in the background provided a soothing music that relaxed Akira. It was another world, a place away from the job that afforded him a paycheck, while remaining invisible.

'Why are you still in this job, Akira?' his father had asked him with a slight shake of the head. This was the mannerism he had given his son, generations merging through one shared trait. Akira would also shake his head when he was dumbfounded. 'You don't create anything…why don't you come and work in the izakaya with me?'

Akira did not want to return to the after-school job of his childhood. He did not want to serve people he knew. He remembered the searing embarrassment when his classmates giggled behind their hands as his father snapped at him relentlessly. Akira did not want the smell of hot oil in his hair that refused to budge even after scrubbing his scalp with the strong-smelling shampoo that was meant to leave his hair smelling of forest pine. Nothing could wipe the smell of Nankotsu from him, that much-loved crispy fried chicken cartilage. It was what everyone wanted with their drinks, but he hated it almost as much as the Tsukemono his mother made herself. The jars of pickled vegetables lined the counter in front of his father who stood front and centre, entertaining the regulars with just the right amount of wit and restraint. The jars were lit up like wondrous candy, but once opened, the sharp pickling would fill his nostrils, holding each cell captive until he was forced to blow his nose to clear some of it away. Akira was sure other children had better smells to contend with. He found himself sniffing his clothes constantly, forcing his mother to call him 'Buraddohaundo' (Japanese for bloodhound).

As he soaped and rinsed himself, he realised how comical he must have looked, sitting on the tiny plastic stool in front of a small mirror barely large enough for him to see himself in. There was nothing glamorous or even pretty about this place. Everything was functional. From the shower head above him, to the two taps that were spotless, wiped clean by the staff who were already hunched over from years of cleaning. He wanted to shave, but realised he was late already, having stayed longer in the office to finish a graph for the next meeting. He was the king of graphs. He colour-coded his way into his boss' good graces even though he knew he could be easily replaced. There was a line of men waiting to replace him if he slipped up. When he sank onto the tiled step in the pool of hot water, he sighed softly. There was a hum of a motor running in the background that provided just the right amount of noise to blend out the traffic. The conversation around him was hushed, but animated. It was a difficult balance, but one that always surprised him in the bath house. When he opened his eyes, he saw the men, all in various stages of ageing, some healthy with skin taut and line-free, others with dark spots on their faces and eyes that appeared sleepy under the unforgiving fluorescent light. They were all equal here, seeking the same distance from the city they lived in and yet were never fully able to leave behind.

After sitting in the pool for a while, he decided he would shave after all. He sat down on his plastic stool and wondered why he did not feel self-conscious about being this naked. All that covered his torso was a thin towel and the moisture had turned it transparent as he rinsed his body. As he closed his eyes, he inhaled a deep smell of jasmine. He opened his eyes quickly as the almost buttery scent hit him and, breaking with convention, he turned to look at the man sitting next to him. He was rubbing an orange bar of soap across his body in rough strokes, and for a second Akira held his breath. He half expected to turn around and see the Cow Brand blue and white package sitting on the sink like it had in his home when he was a child. His father would leave the box that still had a strong floral scent trapped inside, standing on the wet kitchen sink until it fell into itself like a newspaper left in the rain. Akira's mother would moan when she discovered the paper pulp next to her toothbrush, but her scolding was in vain. These were the things he missed most. These were the memories of argument tied forever with a sense of longing in his mind.

The man turned slightly when he noticed Akira staring. It took a moment before the inevitable awkwardness filtered into their shared space, like a strong and determined shadow on a sunny day that blocked out the heat of the sun. It forced a shiver over Akira's back and he smiled meekly before saying, 'My father used to use Aobako soap too. Sorry.'

He expected the man, old enough to have been his father, to look away out of embarrassment and irritation, but instead he said, 'Your father had good taste.' There was a tone of recognition there. 'I have been using this soap all my life, as did my father. He worked in the soap factory in Yasuda.'

Akira looked away quickly, aware of the kindness and being totally unprepared for it. He thought he would have been ignored, or worse, reported for behaving inappropriately. He could not imagine being banned from the sento. He thought of the alternative, using his own bathroom, the one that remained spotlessly clean because every morning he would pack his plastic basket with his toiletries before heading out to work. He thought about his mother insisting they visit the bath house together.

'Oh, come on…I hate going alone,' she had said, almost pleadingly.

She thought she could take over from his father who had collapsed four months ago, clutching at his chest with eyes wide like a balloon fish. Akira knew his refusal hurt her, but she could not replace his father. She could not sit in the water with him and talk in a soothing tone about the izakaya, the soaring price of tuna or the latest wave of children wanting to do something as perverse as photograph their food. Akira would now have to sit alone in the pool and have only the tide of memory, opaque and clear in patches, to keep him company.

When he was dressing in front of the open locker door, he looked up, noticing the man from the wash basin eyeing him curiously. Before he could say anything, the man pushed a small box into his hand and pressed his fingers around it.

'You should carry on the tradition,' he said as he eyed the expensive bodywash bottle in Akira's locker. 'This soap will keep you younger than that.'

4

Akira knew that his cheeks were pink now, mimicking the blossoms outside the front door in their intensity. He did not have to open his palm to know that it was a blue and white box with the iconic black and white cow in the centre. He smiled at the man who was overstepping the demarcated boundary with this act of compassion. Before he could say thank you, the man turned and put on his flat cap, signalling the end of their interaction.

Four hours later, after too many street corners and endless pedestrians moving like animated cuckoo clock figurines, Akira found himself outside his parents' apartment house. He looked up and saw a light still burning in the kitchen window. He rang the doorbell quickly, a quick burst of sound that made a dog bark in the distance. He heard his mother's voice above him and looked up at the first balcony to find her leaning over the side. The buzzer sounded a few seconds later and he ran up the first flight of stairs.

After he had finished the first cup of tea, he caught her looking at him.

'What is wrong?' she asked with clear concern. 'Won't your girlfriend be worried about where you are?'

She would not refer to Kiko by name. Saying it out loud would mean acknowledging that her son was living with a woman out of wedlock. Akira knew the archaic shame would be too much for a woman with her background, a woman who still had the same hairstyle after forty years.

'I know you have been waiting for me to decide about the lease,' he said slowly as he looked at the tiny porcelain cup. It was so tiny that it looked miniature, like part of a children's tea set. 'I know I have been dragging my feet.'

'It's fine.'

'No, it is not,' he said firmly. 'I have been acting like only I lost him.'

He did not want to look up from the table. He was sure it would set her off, start the crying that would prove impossible to stop. How many tears were enough for one death? How many had she shed for the man who was the centre of everything? Akira saw the neat pile of bills, the way the apartment still looked the same. What would they do if his father walked in and started laughing, pointing at them as he hunched over, saying between tight breaths that it was all a joke, that he was alive after all? How cruel would that be?

'I will take over the izakaya.'

'You have a job. Your father would understand.'

'Yes, but I wouldn't.'

Later when he left the apartment he stood outside on the street and looked up at the night sky. Beyond the star formations was a sense of peace, a rare and quiet moment when the city slept in the wake of his decision that would have made his father smile in silent recognition. As Akira walked around the corner he stopped as the scent of jasmine suddenly swam in the air around him like the brush of a hand that felt only familiar.

Mabel Mulvaney is Writing a Book

Once upon a time there was a book inside Mrs. Mabel Mulvaney which was itching to get out. It'd been occupying a dusty corner of Mabel's brain since 2002 when inspiration struck whilst browsing around Sainsbury's homeware department. Mabel had even decided on a title for her literary debut - 'Stickleback'. She purchased a lined hardback notebook with marble end-papers and, once home, opened it at its pristine first page. 'Chapter One' Mabel wrote. She chewed the end of her biro, checked her emails, refilled the bird feeders and put on a load of washing.

Later that day Mabel settled down again with notebook and pen, intent on crafting an opening sentence that'd be a gateway to a world of wonder. But words proved elusive. After ten minutes with the biro's nib poised millimetres from the page, Mabel's son trailed into the sitting room, reeking of teenage angst and Lynx body spray. The notebook was cast aside, unsolicited good advice was offered, and money for a takeaway pizza accepted. No sooner had the son sloped off to order a deep-crust pepperoni than Mabel's husband arrived home, bearing news of Tony and Claire's impending divorce. The notebook, briefly picked up, was put aside again. Mabel rummaged in the freezer for something for dinner. A curry was popped in the microwave to ping twelve minutes later while Mabel was on the phone to Claire.

The following day passed in a haze of household chores, dental appointments and the trauma of taking a bad-tempered cat to the vet. As she lay in bed that evening Mabel decided she needed a plan if 'Stickleback' was ever to be written. Two thousand words a day. That, Mabel thought with confidence, was perfectly do-able. Why, she'd get up an hour earlier than usual each day and knock out those 2,000 before breakfast. Mabel fell asleep and dreamt of rave reviews. A slimmer version of herself gracefully accepted an award while Margaret Atwood looked on with barely concealed envy, and Hilary Mantel offered congratulations through gritted teeth.

Mabel awoke to the alarm clock's insistent ringing. She silenced it and rolled over in bed, reluctant to leave the duvet's cosy cocoon. Maybe an early start wasn't a good idea after all. She went back to sleep. Mabel made a mental note to find time during the day instead, but that didn't happen. It might've, if the washing machine hadn't broken down, leaving her to lug a fortnight's worth of clothes and towels to 'Soapy Suds'. Then there were nametapes to sew into the youngest son's P.E. kit, and the sponge to bake for her sister-in-law's charity coffee morning. (Not that Sarah was grateful. 'I see you've made your coffee cake. Again.')

Deciding 2,000 words had been overly optimistic, Mabel settled on a daily count of 1,000. It'd take a bit longer to write, but she'd get there. Mabel used the calculator function on her phone, 1000 words x 365. Goodness, that was a lot! It'd be a doorstep of a novel.

The next day Mabel cleared a space on the dining table, placed on it her notebook and pen, and sat down, hopes high. Mabel underlined 'Chapter One'. She made a cup of tea and ate digestives. She smoothed the cat's fur and wondered if she dared try clipping Sparky's claws again after the disastrous last attempt that'd ended in a trip to A&E. Mabel turned another page in her notebook and wrote 'Synopsis' before remembering she'd hidden a multipack of KitKats at the back of the saucepan cupboard.

After three days and little progress Mabel thought she needed to be more business-like in her approach to writing. The notebook was put in a drawer. A desk and office chair were ordered and duly delivered. Mabel assembled the desk, which took longer than expected, and placed her laptop on its surface. She arranged a Jenga block of Post-It Notes and stuck a motivational poster on the wall that urged her to remember how a journey of a thousand miles began with a single step. She pinned up a calendar and rethought her plan. Five hundred words a day. Mabel tapped at her phone's calculator, 500 x 365. Not quite a doorstep, but still chunky enough. Opening a blank document on Word, Mabel typed 'Chapter One'. She opened another document and typed 'Synopsis'. Mabel made a cup of tea.

She was certain over the next week that significant progress with 'Stickleback' would be made. But there was the frustrating weekend away at her mother's. The endless dismal phone calls with Claire. The spring bulbs that needed planting. (Oh, why did she give in to 3 for 2 on sacks of daffodil bulbs?) Before she knew it, supermarket aisles were full of tinsel and panettone, and friends were smiling smugly, their Christmas shopping not only purchased but already wrapped. The festive season passed in a whirl of frantic activity and enforced jollity. Five pounds heavier and full of New Year's resolutions Mabel removed the old desk calendar and pinned up a new one.

1st January, a new start.

250 words a day.

'Stickleback,' she thought, here we come.

The following Christmas, five pounds still nestling around her waistline, and joined by two or three more, Mabel did what several newly purchased self-help books urged her to do. She reviewed her year gone by. The false starts, the literary dead ends. The intended word count that'd finally dwindled into nothing. Mabel took down the motivational poster that'd hung over her desk, crumpled it up and pushed it into the recycling bin. Slamming a self-help book shut with a resounding thwack, Mabel lobbed it into the bottom of the hall cupboard. She ate a box of Jaffa Cakes, watched 'Brief Encounter' and enjoyed a good cry. Next year, Mabel thought. There was always next year.

On Cortez Street

It was February and it was cold, and we had been drinking most of the day - we, being me and my college pals, Bentley and Polwinter. We had decided to skip our lectures and spend the day in the bars along the docks. You might say we were rich kids slumming it - many people would have said that, and worse - hanging out with the stevedores and the hawkers and the prostitutes. I say hanging out with - apart from when we were buying drinks or to say excuse me, we didn't really speak to anyone else. I suppose people knew we didn't belong down there.

At some point in the proceedings we started talking about what we were going to do when our courses finished, which at that time was a matter of months away. Bentley, like his father, was headed for the law, although without any great enthusiasm. It was just what happened with men in his family, they studied law, then they worked in law until they retired or died in the job. Polwinter was returning to New Hampshire - or was it Vermont, I get mixed up with those places up there - where he would marry his sweetheart and run the farm that had been in his family for two-hundred-and-fifty years.

Me - I didn't have things laid out so neatly, there was no long family tradition I was expected to follow. I had a vague idea that I might make films - it was what my brother was doing - but first I wanted to travel, to see something of the world before I got serious. I already had an allowance, so I didn't expect to starve. I told Bentley and Polwinter that I wanted some adventures before I was ready for all of that adult stuff, I didn't want to go straight into it.

After four or five hours of solid drinking, we wanted to

move on, and we had the idea to go someplace we hadn't been before. Although we had lived in the city for coming up three years, none of us were from there. We knew the areas around the campus and the better bars and restaurants in the centre. But these outer places were a mystery. Polwinter said, 'How about we go up Cortez Street?'

I said to him, 'Are you crazy?'

'Why not?' he said. 'We've never been up there before. We want to go someplace we've never been, don't we? Bentley?'

Bentley, who was by this time drinking brandy with his beers, said, 'I'm game. There's bound to be some cool bars up there. Why not?'

'Why not?' I repeated. 'You know why not. It's - you know - a black area.'

Which it was. I wasn't saying anything outrageous or that people could take offence at. Cortez Street, and the streets around it, was a place of fearsome legend. It was known for its crime, its broken windows, its addictions, and its hopelessness. It was not predominantly black as they sometimes say. It was black. White people hadn't lived there since before the war. It was said that only black cops patrolled the area, white cops weren't welcome.

I had nothing personal against black people; the truth was I barely knew any. And when it came down to it, me and my pals would probably have had every sympathy for them if we thought about it, and we would wish there was more we could do. But what? We were up against history as much as they were. So no, I didn't think it was a great idea.

'I thought you wanted some adventure,' Bentley said. 'You just said so, barely an hour ago.'

'I didn't necessarily mean that kind of adventure.'

'What you scared of? You think your lily-white skin's going to get contaminated?'

'Yeah, what's the worst that can happen?' Polwinter said. 'We get called Whitey?' He put on a cartoon black accent: 'Hey Whitey, what yo' white ass doin' roun' dese parts?' Bentley thought that was hilarious. He and Polwinter were laughing so hard that people looked.

So, we had one more drink, I bought a fresh packet of Chesterfields from the machine, and we walked a half-a-mile along the river, crossing on Brakeman's Drive. Fifty yards up Cortez Street and it felt like another world. There was nobody around. 'Where the hell is everybody?' Bentley asked. Places were boarded up, doors were hanging off hinges, it looked like a bomb had gone off. There were a few people further up and they looked at us as if we were the first white people they had ever seen. I started to feel my whiteness and wanted to rub it off. Someone shouted something from a balcony, but I couldn't make it out. It wasn't friendly though, I knew that.

'There's a bar up ahead there,' Bentley said.

'I'm not so sure about this,' I said.

'What do you mean, not so sure? It's what we came for, isn't it?'

'Yeah,' Bentley said. 'It's a free country isn't it? A man can go where the hell he likes for a beer.'

'Ok,' I said. 'A quick one then we're out.'

We could hear the noise from inside as we approached. It was called the Plymouth Tavern and the door was jammed open. Polwinter went in first. As soon as he stepped in a black fellow blocked our way. I could see over his shoulder; there were only black people in there. He said to Polwinter, 'You and your friends take a wrong turn, boy?'

'No, we're just out for a beer, friend,' Bentley said from behind. 'We're not looking for any trouble.'

'You don't need to look for trouble in these parts - friend. Trouble'll find you anyway.'

He pushed Polwinter hard in the chest and we all stumbled back onto the sidewalk. The man and many others followed.

'Ok, thanks for the advice,' I said. 'We'll just be on our way.'

A few of them rushed us and Polwinter went down. I can still hear his head crack on the sidewalk. We started swinging wildly but, way outnumbered, we took far more blows than we landed. One of them landed me a haymaker and shouted, 'That's for Malcolm.' I had no idea what he was talking about and didn't have time to ask. We were saved from more serious trouble when a police car with its siren going raced up the street. The passenger door was opened before it stopped, and a black officer got out with his gun up ready for action.

'Get back, boys. Calm down. What's happening here?'

'We got troublemakers here, man. White boys coming here to make trouble.'

'What's happening?' he asked me, his gun still pointed toward our assailants. 'You here for trouble?'

'Course not. We just...'

'What happened to him?' He was looking at Polwinter, who seemed to be unconscious.

'Happened? We've just been attacked, that's what happened. An unprovoked attack.'

'Get an ambulance,' the officer shouted to his colleague.

'This isn't unprovoked, white boy,' one of the men said. 'You provoked us.'

'Ok, ok,' the officer said. 'Let's break it up. Go back to your business.'

'Is that it?' I asked, braver in the proximity of the police. 'They attack us for no reason and then just go back to their business? Look at this.' I pointed down to Polwinter, who was by then sitting up and making hangover sounds. When Polwinter asked what was happening, Bentley knelt and told him. 'Steady there, Polwinter, we just had a bit of a dispute. We're just waiting for help.'

'Come on,' the officer said. 'Split it up.'

The black fellows gave us further insults and shoves before they went back inside. We hung around until an ambulance came for Polwinter. Bentley went with him. The officer told me to get in the car. 'Let's get you out of here,' he said.

When I slid into the back seat, there was a young black kid already in there. He was handcuffed. He gave me a surprised look but didn't say anything.

The cop driving was white. Without looking back he said, 'Bad time for a white kid to be on Cortez. Bad time anytime, but bad now.'

'Bad? Why? Why now?'

'Why? You not hear?'

'Hear what?'

The kid chuckled.

'Malcolm's been shot,' the black officer said. 'You not hear that?'

'Malcolm who?' I asked.

The cops laughed and the black one whooped, and the kid smiled at me and shook his head slowly, as if at my idiocy.

'Malcolm who?' the black cop repeated. 'Is that a sane question from an educated guy? Malcolm X, that's who. He got shot.'

'I see,' I said, although I didn't. 'I'm sorry to hear that.'

'Yeah well,' the black cop said. 'Not everybody liked him. But for the brothers round here, he could do no wrong in their eyes. Remember how you and your folks felt when Kennedy was shot?'

I didn't remember, no.

'Like I say, I'm sorry to hear it.'

'Yeah well, that's why they're so riled up. That's what you walked into.'

'I'll be more careful next time,' I said, with what I had intended to be an undertone of sarcasm.

'If I was you,' the white cop said, not detecting the undertone, 'I would make sure there is no next time. We might not be so close when we're called, next time.'

Ok, I've got the message,' I said.

'You got a cigarette, mister?' the kid asked. He was looking at me like a watcher of birds might look at a bird not seen before.

I opened the Chesterfields and placed one in his handcuffed hand. As he put it to his mouth for me to light, he didn't take his eyes off me.

'Open the window back there if you need to smoke.'

I leaned across him to open his window then I opened mine and lit up.

'Thanks,' he said.

'Where do you need to be?' the driver asked me.

'Just drop me at a transit line. I need to get back to the university.'

The kid, who was having to raise both hands to smoke, said, 'You can drop me there as well.'

'Sure thing,' the black cop said.

They stopped at Singer Street station. 'Your stop.'

The kid said, 'You think you could spare another one of those before you go?'

Stupidly, I was expecting him to get out; of course, he wasn't. I gave him the packet, which had eighteen left in.

'Oh man, all these, thanks. You're ok.'

'What's your name? I asked him.

'Me? My name? Its Eric. Eric.'

I gave him a thumbs up as I went into the station, and he held his tied hands up. I suddenly felt the cold; a freezing wind was blowing along the river. I needed to get back to my room at the campus.

I've no idea what became of Bentley and Polwinter. I didn't see much of them after that, and we were soon gone our different ways. I guess they'll be doing ok. Of course, they will. I know Cortez Street has changed; I know someone who rents out apartments there. He tells me the Plymouth Tavern is now a gallery.

And Eric, what happened to him? It wasn't looking good for him back then; he looked too comfortable in the back of that car. I hope he enjoyed the Chesterfields. And I hope that that one act might have turned things round for him. A packet of Chesterfields, two missing, meant zero to me, but to him it might have meant the world. Maybe I'm kidding myself, but I like to think that small acts of kindness might have that effect, one kind act begetting another and so on and so forth, like dominoes falling into each other around the whole of the world.

Anyway, when I think back to then, which is a seldom thing, I think of Eric a lot more than I think of Bentley and Polwinter. Although I hope that things turned out ok for them also.

Mo

'You might want to know that I'm dying,' Mo told me. 'If you felt like saying goodbye, I have some time this weekend.'

I hadn't seen her in – what, fourteen years? And the attitude dripping from every syllable reminded me why.

'I'll come first thing Saturday,' I said. And that was the end of the conversation.

My sat-nav predicted three hours to the Beeston flat where she'd once been at her happiest, and where I'd been happy enough living with her. Before Lindsay. Before everything fell apart.

My glasses misted as I got into the car. Rain hammered on the windscreen. Stuck in traffic outside Oxford, memories swarmed like midges. Our constant diet of left-over sandwiches. Mo telling me she was getting married, then two days later denying she'd ever said it. Mr Potter laughing with embarrassment when the playing card failed to float and spin in mid-air. Mo railing against the university students who bought their lunches from her in the canteen. Their hairstyles, their manners – though she could hardly talk about manners.

'Why do you call her Mo?' Lindsay asked, early in our relationship. 'Because she's so small?'

'No,' I said. 'Mo is what everyone calls her. It's what she prefers.'

'Didn't you ever just say mum?'

'She wouldn't allow it. It was Mo or nothing at all.'

Thinking about it, the way Mo confided in me suggested she'd rather have had a friend than a daughter. Like her assessment of Mr Potter's sexual prowess, delivered one breakfast time when I was all of ten years old.

'The effort near enough kills him,' she told me. 'And quite

frankly, I don't know why he bothers.'

Mr Potter was kind to me, and I liked him. Mo's other 'male friends' were much younger and largely ignored me. One or two were twenty years younger than Mo. She was pretty youthful in those days and lied brazenly about her age.

When I went to university myself, Mo felt threatened. She never visited me on campus, and when she met Lindsay she withdrew even further. Something about him got to her, his ability to talk confidently about any subject maybe. In Mo's mind, Lindsay was your typical arrogant student, and responsible for our relationship falling apart. But the writing was already on the wall. In fluorescent paint.

The final set-to happened the Christmas after we got married. Lindsay and I divided those few days between Mo and his divorced parents. How Mo hated being allocated her portion of our time! And then Lindsay made a disparaging remark about Mo's slender grasp of politics. Feeling humiliated sent Mo into a fury. A week later she announced that Lindsay was never setting foot in her flat again. I told her Lindsay and I came together or not at all. 'That's it, then,' she said. Three small words to end a mother-daughter relationship. It felt more of a relief than a loss.

Stupidly, I worried that as soon as she heard Lindsay had left me for another woman, Mo would tell me she'd been right about him all along. I even thought about turning the car around, heading home, just to deny her the pleasure.

I parked across the road, braced myself, and undid the gate latch. The all too familiar pathway stood before me, the small patch of garden to the right with a discarded television-set encircled by weeds.

I rang the bell. Hearing nothing, I clattered the letterbox. The door opened slowly, and there was Mo in a sleeveless summer frock, her hair gleaming an unnatural brown. She looked up at me, though every feature of her face was turned down. The lines at the edges of her mouth were scored like B-roads running south on a map.

'You should probably come in,' she said, as if there were other options.

I followed her down the dark hallway, into the lounge. Mo gestured towards the small table, the table where I'd eaten meals with her and whoever happened to be knocking around at the time.

Rather than sitting too, Mo remained standing, the side of her face angled towards the far corner of the room.

'You look well,' I ventured.

'So, you don't believe I'm dying.'

The yawning chasm of time, the unspoken grievances, the distrust between us, were like three additional guests shuffling around the room, wincing with discomfort.

The leaden silence was punctuated only by her heavy breathing.

'Of course I believe you.'

'It's my heart, if you're the least bit interested.'

I nodded. She didn't look like she was about to keel over but I wasn't going to argue. 'Life hasn't been easy for me either,' I said.

Mo harrumphed and disappeared into the kitchen.

I looked around. No pictures, no photos, nothing from my childhood. Only Monty, the crystal woodpecker, standing on some papers on the mantelpiece. The place was a shell. Mo always had been ruthless in discarding possessions as well as people.

She returned with a pot of tea, two cups, and a plate of gingersnaps. My mouth watered. Gingersnaps were my absolute childhood favourite. I dared to hope she'd remembered and bought them specially.

This time Mo sat down too, hesitantly, as if I might have booby-trapped her chair while she was out of the room.

We sipped our tea without speaking. Mo dunked a biscuit and crammed half into her mouth. We munched while her small eyes scrutinised me.

'Still working in books?'

My first job was in publishing. But I'd changed track even before moving in with Lindsay.

'Not for a while,' I said. 'I'm in personnel. For an energy company. I have my own team.'

Mo stuck her bottom lip out, a gesture I associated with her being profoundly unimpressed.

'Still married to Lindsay?'

'No,' I replied.

'Am I a grandmother?'

'No,' I said again.

I thought I'd give Mo time to digest these two pieces of information. But she didn't need it.

'I never thought much of him,' she said.

I nodded. 'I'll bet you're working in catering still?'

'Catering!' she snorted. 'Is that what you call selling sandwiches? And I'm about to drop dead, remember?'

'Sorry,' I said. 'I didn't think.'

Mo rolled her eyes.

'Come on, Mo,' I said. 'We might have a conversation if you'd give it half a chance.'

Mo considered this. 'And what's this conversation to be about?'

I could have started by asking, 'Who was my father?' But that would have been controversial. I suspected he was from the university. A lecturer or professor. Someone with his own room. My fantasy was that there'd been a scandal and he'd been forced out of his post.

'I used to feel like a disappointment to you,' I said, realising immediately this could be incendiary too.

She didn't fly off the handle. But she didn't contradict me either.

'Like you'd rather I'd been someone else,' I pushed my luck a little further.

'I always wanted a son,' Mo admitted.

This was news. It made sense too.

'I know things weren't perfect around here,' she added.

For Mo this was massive. Were we actually making progress?

'I appreciate that, Mo,' I said. 'And I know you did what you could.'

There was another pause which Mo filled by refreshing our cups.

'What happened to Mr Potter?' I asked.

'Him! I'm surprised you ask about him,' she laughed.

Mo laughing was not something I remembered happening often. Perhaps when she read me poems at night, those nonsense poems by Edward Lear, back when I was very small. That felt like another life. Mo was quite a reader, in her own way.

'I'm just curious,' I said. 'Mr Potter used to show me magic tricks, that's all. But they never seemed to work.'

'There wasn't much about Mr Potter that was magic,' Mo said.

I smiled, recollecting her description of Mr Potter's sexual prowess.

'Anyway, he's been dead years. Got a letter from his daughter. Inviting me to the funeral.'

I felt a pang of sadness at this mild man's passing. 'Did you go?'

'Why would I have done that?'

'I don't know. To pay your respects maybe. For old times' sake. I might have gone if you'd told me about it.'

Mo looked at me steadily over her glasses. 'If this is about scoring points, you may as well leave.'

I took a slow breath. One step forward, two steps back.

'What would you like to talk about?' I asked.

Rising from her seat, she walked behind me. Papers rustled. A letter fluttered from above me, landing almost in the centre of the table.

I was able to read a few words from where I was sitting. Queen's Medical Centre. Maureen Lambert – d.o.b. Coronary heart disease.

'You want me to read it?'

Mo shrugged. 'If you like.'

I reached for the letter. Scanned it quickly. There were medical terms I wasn't familiar with. But the ending was clear enough. The words jolted me like whiplash. I read them again in case I'd missed something.

'It says you need urgent bypass surgery.'

'That's right.' Mo had sat opposite me again. She was looking down at her lap.

'And that you're refusing to have it.'

'Yes,' she said. As if this could hardly be surprising.

The patient is competent and understands the likely consequences of refusing treatment,' I read aloud. 'What's going on, Mo?'

Mo's tongue ran along her bottom lip. She said nothing.

'*We have discussed her rights to determine her treatment plan and the clear risks involved.* Did they discuss your rights, Mo?'

She was breathing heavily again.

'Did they, Mo?'

'Yes.'

'And?'

'I told him he could stick his by-pass surgery where the sun don't shine.'

'Dear God,' I muttered. 'You didn't say that?'

Mo looked up. 'Of course I did,' she said proudly.

'But you'll die, Mo. Is that what you want? You're only sixty-four for goodness sake.' I'd worked out her age during the long car journey.

'I'm finished,' Mo said.

'No, you're not,' I jumped in. 'The letter says that there's every chance –'

'It's over,' she interrupted. 'There's no point. Not anymore. Even the men have lost interest. And that's probably all I ever had.'

'Well, partners come and go. Look at me. I haven't had one in three years. That's just how it is. But you're still young enough, Mo. You've got plenty of living inside you yet.'

'No one wants me around. No one cares about me.'

It felt like I was being set a test. That she was daring me to contradict her. Was I meant to say I loved her? I was pretty sure I couldn't do it.

'No one cares about me. And that's the truth,' Mo concluded.

She pushed a hand under her glasses and brushed the corner of her eye.

'So why do you think I'm here?' I began. 'Why did I just drive three hours in the pouring rain if I don't care?'

'The will, I should think.'

'Oh, don't be so ridiculous! I don't need your money. I wanted to see you. We've had difficult times. But isn't that what it's about? Getting through those? You may be an old battle-axe, but I don't want you to die.'

At some point she'd got up and wandered over to the window. A shaft of sunlight caught her hair, making it gleam brighter.

'He said it could happen any time,' she said.

'Is this why you've brought me here? Why you've drawn me in again. To torment me?'

'Old battle-axe,' she laughed. 'I hope that goes on my tombstone.'

'You're not dying yet, Mo. We're going to tell him you've changed your mind.'

'It's brightening up outside,' Mo said.

'We can email the consultant today,' I said. 'Mo! You're not answering me.'

'Is that what you want?' she asked.

'Yes, it's what I bloody well want. And I'm pretty sure it's what you want too.'

'Well, I suppose. But you're writing the words. And I don't do email.'

Verity and Justine

In 2012 a statue measuring more than 20m in height (66ft) was raised at the harbourside in Ilfracombe, North Devon, the gift of artist Damien Hirst. Called Verity, the figure is a pregnant woman forged in stainless steel and bronze, holding a sword aloft. She clutches the scales of justice and is perched on a pile of books. Controversy surrounds the work as internal organs on one side of the stomach are revealed.

Justine pulled up the hood of her duffle coat and hunkered down onto the bench beside the harbour, trying to diminish the sting of the wind which was blowing straight towards her up the Bristol Channel. It tugged tendrils of her hair, grasping the red strands, creating a veil across her eyes. The wind made the waves jagged and cross, similar to her mood. She wished she could crash onto the rocks and throw spray high to ease the boil of feelings in her head.

She pushed the fourth finger of her left hand through the toggle loop of her coat. The hoop was slightly small and made her finger red as she tried to remove it. A wedding or even an engagement ring might stop people staring at her as if she were a monster. Stop them judging her with the accusation, 'Guilty!'

At this time of the day, her friends would be hunched over their desks, confined. But though she'd always made out she'd hated school, she wished she was there now.

Even with the wind moving the air, the smell of burger grease and fish hung over the harbour. It made her feel queasy. She chewed a fingernail.

The statue of Verity rose twenty metres, dominating the harbour, her pose striding towards the distant horizon with purpose. Justine observed Verity as she did most afternoons, absorbing the serene gaze of the statue hoping it would rub off on her. She smoothed the fabric of her coat with her cold fingers and sighed. Beneath her touch, the baby kicked. A jut of elbow or foot jabbed her under the ribs, and she gasped. It hurt.

Verity remained composed and still, without the anxiety of childbirth to come. Half her belly was exposed like a 3D diagram from one of the pre-natal pamphlets Justine had been given. Verity's moulded babe was motionless, whereas Justine's bump kicked all the time.

What was to come terrified Justine. The challenge of how that big baby was going to squeeze out of her body. She shuddered under her coat.

The arrival of Verity had caused consternation. Her parents had been on the critical end. 'But it's ugly. Not suitable for Ilfracombe.' And they'd tutted and shaken their heads and spoken in loud whispers in the high street shops to vent their dismay. Justine felt she'd had a similar press. How brazen she'd been and, now she was well into the third trimester, how outrageous her behaviour was.

Still, her parents had let her stay, even if the atmosphere at home was different. It was quieter, the conversation muted. The bulk of Justine's pregnancy was a barrier between them. They walked around her like the tourists did around Verity, giving her curious glances, unsure what to make of her. That's why Justine liked to sit here and have a one-sided conversation with the statue. Everything about her displayed strength and fortitude: the stride forward, the head held high, the sword in the air and the scales of justice. Justine had kept that image in her head when one of the nurses at the surgery had suggested she have an abortion. Imagining she held a sword, she'd filled her short frame with as much resolve as she could and told them, 'My baby's a living thing. I won't murder it!'

She nibbled a fingernail. She'd had false nails the night of the school prom. They'd looked great; silver with little stars. Ty had caressed her hand pressing the palm with his thumb. His touch had made her shiver. She'd been flattered when he'd picked her over other prettier girls. Beside the red hair, she was plain, average. Though, that evening, she'd felt beautiful. Her mum had helped her choose the green dress. 'It suits your colouring,' she'd said.

Ty had pulled her outside to escape the crowded, sweaty atmosphere of the school hall. The cool night air wrapped itself around her. As Justine took a breath it filled her, carrying a thrill around her body. She could hear her heart beating, sounding loud above the throb of the disco music inside. They'd run down to the harbour, laughing. She'd kicked off her shoes and the cold paving pressed under her feet, making her aware of gravity, keeping her on the ground. Every sensation was novel. On the jetty, Ty had pressed her up against the wall. Her head was filled with alcohol and excitement. Even if Verity had called out a warning, Justine knew she wouldn't have stopped to consider the possible consequence of her actions. The harbour lights were spinning around her, dancing on the water, making her dizzy. Ty's kisses were warm and salty and a new sensation. She could hear the wash of the waves, and everything seemed brighter and better than ever before.

Now she wasn't average. She was a statistic.

Yes, she agreed with her parents that she'd been stupid. But one-night stands in a boring town were hardly a new occurrence. And yes, she was young, but later she'd get a job. She'd manage with a bit of support. At first her mum had just cried, unable to say anything and her father shook his head and returned to his study to smoke. Their attitude had been similar to the day Verity was craned into place. Her mother saying nothing but looking shocked that it had gone ahead. Her father had said it was 'demeaning to women'. But Justine couldn't see why the figure was any more demeaning than her mother cleaning for other people all day and then coming home to make sure tea was on the table. Dad wouldn't think to cook instead.

Now Justine felt old. She slept awkwardly in her single bed as her belly expanded. Her childhood stuffed toys fell off the edge and hid behind the headboard. She awoke with grey bags under her eyes, feeling middle-aged, seeing her features in the mirror frown at her like her mother's.

That's why she came to the harbour, she felt as though she fitted in. People would wash up there if they had nowhere else to go. They walked past with vacant eyes, moving without direction as if disappointed with life. She wished her coat was bright - green maybe, or red, to lift the mood of the day. But the duffle was grey and too large. None of her maternity clothes fitted properly; they were all bought from charity shops in large sizes.

Today was very grey, so everything was even grimmer. Grey sea, grey gulls, the rocks around the harbour black. Verity was grey as well but with a cast of green on her bronze skin and still magnificent. Justine imagined her plaited hair would be red like hers. Once, Justine had been cast as the figure of Britannia in a school play. Red hair brushed into ripples. With her cardboard shield and sword, she'd felt invincible. It seemed like a long time ago. Her mother had once said she should be an actress. That was a long time ago too. Now all she could expect was disappointment.

Two months later:

Justine was striding out along the harbour, head held high, her hair in a braid down her back, like Verity's. The sun was shining, and she felt strong and comfortable. No more kicking under her ribs. She was wearing a bright T shirt and leggings, which had been bought by her mum. Ahead of her, her mother pushed the pram; it was an expensive one her parents had revealed the day after the birth. They continued to surprise her. Her dad was even trying to give up smoking.

Her mother was smiling, humming a tune, as she pushed the pram with pride through the afternoon crowd. The baby's head with its flick of red hair was just visible under the blanket his grandma had knitted.

'No wonder Verity looks so calm,' Justine said to her mum. 'She doesn't have to go through that horrible, painful giving birth bit!'

Her mother smiled at her. 'Well, that pain will fade, and look, you've got a gorgeous baby at the end of it.' She leaned forward making cooing noises to her grandson.

The familiar smells of frying and fish were in the air, but Justine felt encased and protected in the new scent of motherhood. Never had a fragrance been more satisfying.

The gulls were chatty, circling in the air, hovering on the light breeze. The crowd around Verity was busy, the warmth of the day bringing out tourists and locals. A few of them turned to look at the red-headed baby being pushed past.

Justine found a place on a bench. Her mother sat beside her and rocked the pram, talking to the baby about the sound of the waves, the boats and the gulls.

'You know Justine, I didn't like that statue at first.' She reached over to grasp Justine's hand, and squeezed it. 'But now I'm getting used to her.'

Justine looked up at the statue's face. She hadn't been certain before but now she could see that Verity was smiling.

Matchsticks and Zombies

Nine across: one of seven and not too pleased about it (six letters).

Bill looked up from his crossword at the new arrivals in the residents' lounge. That was Doris's granddaughter, Kara or something, and he supposed the sullen-looking child with her must be Doris's great-grandson. For goodness sake, look at him! Sprawled out on the chair, completely ignoring Doris, with a face like he's found a penny and lost a pound. Typical of today's kids: rude, arrogant and ungrateful. It annoyed Bill no end that over the eighty-four years he'd been on this planet, kids seemed to get more and more given to them yet were more miserable for it.

He studied the boy over the top of his Daily Mail. About ten years old, he reckoned, ridiculous baseball cap worn the wrong way round (shouldn't be worn at all indoors), jeans and a black top with a skull printed on it, perfect for wearing to an old people's care home, that'll cheer us all up! His mother is telling him to stop kicking his foot against the table; these must be the infamous £58 trainers Doris was on about - £58 and they're not even proper shoes. Doris said his mother bought them for his birthday; £58 for a pair of glorified plimsolls, it beggared belief - and he was still kicking the table.

Bill remembered his school shoes, second-hand and too big for him, he'd had to wear two pairs of socks. He polished them every day and Lord help him if they got scuffed. His only other footwear was a pair of boots with iron studs hammered into them; Bill reckoned they probably weighed as much as he did. He loved those boots; they were his footie boots, his tree climbing boots, his army boots when they went off to the woods to play war. He doubted the fancy trainers would have lasted a week.

That was the problem with the brats these days, they never got out and did anything. The boy was now hunched over some electronic game thing that probably cost as much as a small car. He could at least talk to his great-grandmother, but no, he just sat there ignoring everyone. Bill tried to concentrate on the clues, but the boy's presence, and the rhythmic clunk of £58 trainer on table leg, was causing him no end of annoyance. Now he could hear him asking his mother if he could have money to get a can of Coke from the vending machine in the lobby.

'No,' his mother said, 'you've just had lunch.'

'But I didn't have a drink,' the boy whined.

'Have water then.'

'I don't like water.'

'Don't be silly.'

'But I'm really thirsty.'

Jeez, how that whinging voice grated on Bill's nerves.

'Oh, here you are then,' she said in exasperation. 'When you've got your drink, come and find Granny and me in the garden, we're going to sit in the sun.'

Typical, thought Bill. Today's parents just didn't know how to bring up kids and they spoiled them rotten. She should have given him a clip round the ear, that's what he would have got at that age.

12 across: a man's tale, a subject to study perhaps? (seven letters).

Bill thought back to when he was ten, which would have been 1947. He had lived with his mother on the outskirts of Exmouth, a small town near Exeter on the south coast. His father had been killed soon after the start of the war and Bill had no memories of him. He still had a photograph of his father holding him as a toddler; Bill had grown up with that photo looking down at him from the mantelpiece, but that's all his father had ever been, a stranger in a photograph.

His mother worked as a dressmaker then, and all her

working life. They were always skint, but they got by and were happy. Bill was grateful for everything he had, and he was not the only boy without a father in those dark times. His best mates were Tommy Milton and Henry Banks. They'd play football in the road where he and Tommy lived (Henry lived just round the corner). The highlight of the week was sharing Henry's 'Hotspur' comic on a Saturday morning. He always had chores to do but they still had plenty of time for playing in the nearby woods, building dens and damming up the little stream.

At fifteen he left school and became an apprentice at a local boat builder, and at eighteen he joined the merchant navy. He travelled the world before eventually settling down and marrying his beloved Edith. They were together forty-three years before she passed away; that was some eight years ago. They had tried for a family but were unable to have children; the whole test tube miracle came a little too late for them, and anyway, Edith would say that if the good Lord didn't bless them with children then that was His will. Bill had lived alone for six years but, after a mild stroke, he found he couldn't easily cope, and a place was found for him here at Willow Tree Court.

8 down: a serious disagreement (eight letters).

'WICKED!' Bill was jolted out of his reminiscing by the exclamation behind him.

'Get away from there. Don't touch it!' Bill shouted, drawing disapproving looks from around the room. The boy had materialised in Bill's corner of the room and now took a step back from the meticulously crafted matchstick model of HMS Victory on the low table behind Bill's chair.

'I was only looking,' the boy said sulkily. 'Didn't touch it.'

He looked like he might start crying, and Bill knew he had spoken too harshly.

'It's very delicate,' he said more kindly. 'It's taken me months to build it, I've almost finished... I'm sorry I shouted.'

The boy was looking at the model with a face full of wonder.

'It's sick, just brill, it's got tiny cannons and everything.'

'I've used seventeen thousand matchsticks,' Bill said, warming to his favourite topic, 'and thirty yards of twine.'

'What's yards?'

'Like metres but a bit shorter,' explained Bill with a smile. The boy's obvious enthusiasm was winning him over. 'So, what's your name then?'

'William,' replied the boy. 'What's yours?'

'Hah, William as well, only everyone calls me Bill.'

16 across: what a muddle, that'll break the ice (four letters).

'How did you make those tiny people?' asked William and Bill showed him the craft knife and magnifying glass he used.

'I paint them with this little brush,' explained Bill. 'Don't you ever do Airfix kits with your dad?'

'Haven't got a dad,' William said casually. 'Mum said he ran off before I was born.'

Bill said he was sorry, and William shrugged; the old man knew what it felt like to be asked about a father he'd never known.

'Would you like to help me paint some sailors?'

'Really? That'd be great.'

'You'll have to be careful not to get paint on those fancy shoes,' Bill warned, and was surprised when the boy said it didn't matter because the shoes were a waste of money anyway.

'I don't expect your mother would be pleased to hear you say that.'

'She said they weren't worth what they cost and that I should have saved my gardening money towards a new bike,' William mumbled. 'And she was right.'

'Gardening money?'

'Yeah, I pull out weeds and cut the grass for Mrs Hiscock next door, she's too old to do it herself; she pays me three pounds a week.'

Bill was reconsidering his opinion of this boy; he wasn't

such a bad lad after all.

When his mother and great-grandmother came in a while later the two Williams were huddled over a Gameboy.

'There you are,' she said. 'I wondered where you'd got to.'

'I'm showing Bill how to play Zombie Apocalypse,' her son replied, 'while we wait for the paint to dry.'

'Aargh!' said Bill, frantically pressing buttons while a Zombie chewed off his foot.

'Can we come back next weekend, Mum? Bill said I can help him make the sails.'

'Well... I'm not sure...'

'I'd love to see him,' Bill interrupted, and was surprised to find he meant it. The short time he'd spent with the boy gave him a glimpse of what it would have been like to have had a son.

That evening found Bill deep in thought; the day had taken a very unexpected turn. For some time he had been aware of taking longer and longer over finishing his model, being ever more precise and particular over every detail. He had come to think of it as the last meaningful thing he would do on this earth. When it was finished, he'd decided, there would be nothing left for him to live for, the book of his life was written, and he would be ready to meet his maker. He'd been feeling very low. Then he thought about William, a good lad that might benefit from some 'grandfatherly' advice, and he wondered if there wasn't another chapter in him yet. Perhaps the boy might like to help him build a model Spitfire, and in return, he could show Bill how to get to the second level of 'Zombie Apocalypse'; he was sure he'd nearly made it. He picked up his pen and crossword – one answer eluded him:

18 Across: Zeus' demise brings someone good luck (seven letters).

Bill gave a little satisfied grunt as the solution came to him. Sometimes, he reflected, you just had to look a little harder to see the truth.

Silent Home

He came from a silent home. The family sat at the table, next to the heavy floral curtains, and shared dinner, a pitcher in the middle. His mother's half-open eyes smiled at him, and they used the word, not the kiss, goodnight, before he went to bed in his attic room and switched on the red mushroom-shaped night light clamped to his headboard. Silence was their language. Silence was their every day. Questions waited patiently and didn't dare leave. Why did her eyes turn away when she laughed to herself? Where did she go for those long walks?

He had a vague sense that his parents had lived through a different era, a history he didn't know, that was wrapped up tight and kept apart from the outside world - a history ongoing, that was written into the dark brick of their house, that had lived through two wars, a story that wasn't communicated in words but echoed in the blunt look of their kitchen window above the table. A sense of time had stopped, a clear awareness of absence. It was present in the way his mother had surrendered, and his father stored things for safekeeping. There were family recipes and routines. And if something was communicated to the outside, who would know, who would listen? There was always the ordinary, everyday life.

He learned to speak and understand silence. There was no problem except when others, who weren't familiar with this language, didn't understand. Teachers asked him to speak up in class, to name things early. Friends told him they couldn't read him. He dreaded it, the decision on how to say things. He knew the colours of the moment: blue, red, grey and white. These colours were familiar like the leaves turning red in autumn.

Black silence was rare, black he feared. Like when his father went out to look for his mother, and he stayed alone at the kitchen counter and couldn't make the can opener work. He sat quietly at the table and watched the black birds and imagined them looking down on the steeple of the church nearby, the neighbours small like ants, black.

Another time, he found his mother sitting on the edge of her bed, her hair covering most of her pale face, in stillness, as if her body had gone cold like water over ice, and her eyes asked, Can I go? He was still wearing his hard-shell backpack with the pencil case in the front pocket. He knew a casual response wouldn't do.

He crossed his arms around his chest and tried to breathe evenly, until he couldn't keep himself from answering any more. His arms flung from his body, and the backpack dropped from his shoulders and thumped on the purple bed spread. I am only thirteen, his eyes shouted, and I haven't finished school yet.

When he was older, around fifteen, his mother stopped in the hallway and looked at him. Her hair was still black, and her green eyes snapped to attention. One hand reached for him, wanting something. It was like she hadn't seen him in weeks, maybe years.

'How are you?' she said, her voice soft.

'Fine.' A casual response should do, he thought, confused.

'How's school?'

'Fine.'

'Hungry?'

'A little.'

'Did I ever tell you it took me a long time to learn how to write my name?' She kept her eyes pinned on him.

He looked back at her. They were now the same height. 'No, you didn't.' He imagined his mother as a little girl, black ponytails long enough to be dipped in black ink.

'I was not a very good student.' Her eyes clouded. 'Not like you.'

'In writing?'

'In writing and reading.'

'Will you read to me?' he dared to ask, aware of the newness of his words.

'I read slowly,' she said.

At first, it was a plaintive whisper. Then his mother's voice filled with depth and temperature and wrapped itself around their breaths. They sat on the hard cushions of their sandy beige couch, and he watched her speak, resenting, loving, his eyebrows tight, one knee up to his chest, until he felt that her voice spoke directly to him and a question from a deeper well was being answered.

The story was about a man at sea, and there were long passages about the force of water and the man fighting it. They didn't talk about the story. The sky outside their house got dark, and they drunk in words and voice. Her speech picked up pace, his breath calmed. There was solidity in the sound between them he hadn't expected, a solidity he understood as caring. Then his mother closed the book with a soft thump and smiled. She prepared dinner, he took out the utensils, and when his father came home, they sat down at the kitchen table and ate. Her voice never left again.

He left home, became an engineer in the merchant marines and married, no children. His mother's hair turned white, and her eyes stayed green, and many years later, he rushed to her bed in the ICU, a place he'd never thought of, not for her. She smiled at him faintly and then closed her eyes until the next morning. When they opened again, they asked, Can I go? He didn't know what to answer. There were no more school days or dinners to take care of. He didn't want to make the necessary calls. He didn't want to leave the room. He didn't want to search for words with his mother, and he couldn't tell what colour that moment was. There were only the words that flew from their wet eyes, their language. There were the things that never change. His mother lifted her eyebrows.

'I am here,' he whispered and took her hand. And I don't know life without you. His heart ached. He held his palm over her eyes to shield them from the white florescent light. Together now they floated in the invisible sea, and her face brightened, as if she saw all the beauty, all the promise in him.

'Can I go?' she then mouthed again, tenderly, as if kissing a bird, and the glow in her green eyes implied she knew why. He wanted to say, perhaps. He spoke so quietly, he had to press his mouth to her ear. Perhaps you are not leaving; perhaps you are arriving. And he gently squeezed her hand, and felt her warm palm close around his, and then he heard the release of breath from her half-open lips, before he could even think.

Chaperone

On stage, he is still quite beautiful to me. His eyes are still huge on his face, presumably here to stay into adulthood. His face and his body are still soft with the stockiness of puppy fat, doughy beneath the clothes he now only wears on stage, swathed the rest of the time in Reebok and Adidas when he is at home and out of public view. Last time I collected him he was wearing his sister's Blue Ivy hoodie that I suspect he loves for its softness, and its association with her. His hands seem huge to me now, as they trot through the pre-defined gestures that I - his coach, his director, his ghost-writer, whatever - first drilled into him three years ago when his softness and his wide eyes were real, not the learned last resort of someone whose legitimacy would be forever anchored in the worst twenty minutes of his life. Now he is standing unperturbed in front of a huge photograph of the bloody aftermath of the attack, and now in front of the last photo of him and his four siblings together: his sister crushed in the middle of the unholy trinity of younger brothers she had the bad luck to end up with; he with his fringe too long; the little one - too little to be at school that day and still too small to count really, in the maths of who had suffered - and the boy who died. The utterly unremarkable boy who died; a child made interesting only by his death.

People find two things disconcerting about him, usually. One is his overall physical wellness: his rude health, his sturdy frame, his bright eyes. They cannot join the dots before the dust-covered, half-crushed child in the photographs and the person they see today. I would help them - explain his recovery, that his injuries were not terribly severe, in fact - were it not for the fact that I, too, continue to find his robustness unnerving. The second thing that people assume is that he will be ruined psychologically. They see him standing in front of the terrible photographs, speaking without hesitation or a crack in his voice and they are perturbed. On this point, I oscillate. I made the boy who stands on the stage: gave him his words, his fearlessness, touted him out to the people who'd want him, negotiated his speaker's fees. But each time he speaks, I wait for the crack in his voice, for the head hung, for the stutter and the stop. I never doubted that day would eventually arrive. But so far it has not and, even though I think perhaps I should, I cannot lift the rubble of this work off his chest.

People love him, of course. After he comes off stage, people discreetly stare at him as he gets a glass of water and sits down in the front row. He strides confidently, too good at avoiding their eye for it to be a coincidence. He sits down next to me, the heavy mass of him incongruous with the boy he so recently was: his back too broad for the chair and his arms, more fat than muscle, greedily taking up the whole arm rest between us, though respectfully avoiding the one on the other side. I raise my eyebrows and reach towards my bag, wrestling a Coke out from its depths. This remains his post-talk treat, unchanged since he first came to the country and was shocked and delighted by the range of fizzy drinks, despite initial disappointment in not being able to source Mountain Dew: a US drink that, I suspect, he got used to when it made its way off bases and into nearby villages when he was a child.

When we were in the US last year, I bought him some, but he found it too sweet; the memory of a childhood treat punctured then shrivelled by the reality. Surprised by the treat, his face brightened for a second, and then contorted in disgust. When I looked back at him a moment afterwards, I saw his expression slack with disappointment. Mountain Dew was yet another of the surviving shards of the life he lived before, now slipping away. Even then, I thought: God, this is his whole life - the reliving of memories either involuntarily, or to earn the money his family needs, or to try to do the thing we say we are doing: promote peace, resist the worst in ourselves. Or because the person who holds most of your life in her hands bought you a Mountain Dew and now a thousand fights with your little brother over the last swallow are made meaningless. His days are a series of losses: small, large and endlessly re-lived.

After the session ends and he has drained the Coke, we stand up ready to leave. A few courageous onlookers flock around him, desperate to chat. I steer him through the crowd, explaining that we have to dash away because I have to get him back to school. It's complete nonsense, of course: after he does one of these, he is exhausted and spends the taxi journey to the station and the train journey staring morosely out of the window, hardly talking. It used to bother me - his silence, his taciturn face - but I realised after a few months that this is his default expression more or less constantly, when he isn't in front of an audience, or mugging for Instagram, or engaged in a row with his sister or a game on his phone. Immobile faces are unnerving, of course: I am reminded of the experiment with the babies where their mothers turn away, and the infants become increasingly, heart-wrenchingly desperate to secure their parent's attention. In that scenario, I suppose I am the desperate baby, which is how I used to feel with him: desperate to elicit a smile, or a laugh, or provoke any sort of reaction. But reacting - or the appearance of it - is exclusively reserved for when he is 'on', as far as I can see: on stage, on television, hellbent on impressing a funder he knows someone wants him to impress. I had always assumed his impassivity was a choice when he wasn't visible, but the more I search for any reason that he would continue to do this work - relive the horrors, tolerate the train journeys, exchange pleasantries with American billionaires - the more I suspect that he does it because this is the only time he is able to be animated now. His feelings are there only when he is half-faking it for the conference floor. Stopping the endless circuit of talks and glad-handing might mean they disappeared altogether.

We are walking in front of the conference centre to take a cab, this time. We are not too far from home; I have asked the organisers to fund the drive all the way back to where he lives, in a well-kept three bed terrace that his father - no doubt their cowboy landlord's dream - has steadily restored to habitable from the wreck they initially moved into. When they had first arrived and found the stinking carpets and broken windows, none of them could conceal their horror. But slowly and with almost no help, his father has rebuilt: repainted walls, hung donated mirrors and Koranic verses sent by well-wishers overseas. Painstakingly, his mother washed the carpets by hand: mop and bucket, day after day, until the stench receded and then disappeared completely. His sister helped; the luxuries of uncooperative adolescence denied to her. And the little one carried on as he always did, buffeted from one slightly irritated family member to another, head patted, face stroked, shoved and jostled and teased and permanently in possession of a snack. Getting away with everything, I was once told.

When I arrive at the house, for collections or for returns from conferences, it is always the little one who greets us. He is no longer so tiny, of course, but his relative smallness still carries the day. Somehow his face still breaks open with joy when he sees us approaching from where we've been dropped, as he stands waiting by the windowsill, raised up so he can see further down the road to better anticipate our arrival. When he was really small, he would immediately demand that I lift him up, holding him on my hip like a baby. That happened every time until one day his father caught him and pulled him away. As a toddler he liked my hair, I think: long, easier to access than his mother's and, of course, a strange colour. When his mother was out of the room, he would sometimes pick up my ponytail and pinch the bottom together in his small fingers to make a little brush with the ends of my hair, which he would dust against the dark down on his forearm.

Even now, years later, he is sitting by the window, face on hand, staring down the road waiting for our return. We can see him before he can see us, so we see the moment when he leaps up, shouting no doubt that we are here, racing to open the door so we are welcomed back when we are still several metres down the street. He waits adoringly for the ruffle or the pat from his returning brother and then runs to fetch his mother to speak to me. We exchange a few words - the only words we have really ever exchanged, unfettered by translators - that he has done well again today, that there will be a fee and it will be sent to their family, and that he has not eaten since lunch. She offers me a snack and I sit for a moment, surrounded by the busy joyfulness of the kitchen: the vat of chutney, the sack of rice by the back door, the plates that are always sparkling on the draining board, as if never used. Always she brings me something to eat: warm and spicy, although clearly with the heat tempered for my weakling palette. I eat, without finishing so they know I am serious about leaving, and sit while the little one shows me a new reading book.

Then I leave and return to what still feels to me like my real life even though, quite obviously, this life is the one that I spend more and more time in. I see more of their family than my own. My days carting his Cokes and Quavers around conference halls are outnumbering the days I spend writing speeches for the great and good, or telling Ministers what they already know, but prefer to ignore, about international arms controls. The life that is supposed to be my real life, and my real-real life are no longer remotely adjacent to each other. I am entirely in the slipstream of their ordinary and exceptional life.

The Goddess and the Fire Dancer

There's a beach in Hawaii where an old man in a yellow shirt sits and strums his ukulele. Sometimes he sings along, and sometimes he just plays to himself, picking tunes out of the air.

Sometimes tourists throw coins to him, but more often he's alone with the lovebirds which cluster in the trees above him.

As he plays, he watches the waves break on the shore, and listens to the sounds all around him. He says he can hear the islands breathing, but he says a lot of things like that. He's as black as polished wood, with a bright wrinkled smile, and always beside him is a leather bag.

On this day he's not smiling. He's watchful, and his fingers are hesitant on the strings. The tourists are ignoring him. He's not playing for the crowds today. He's gone somewhere in his head, and his face is as still as a carved statue. He's listening hard today, and he can hear a change. There is a restlessness in the tide. The breeze is fitful and fickle. There are no clouds, but somehow there is a darkness in the day. The air is heavy. Perhaps there will be thunder? Or perhaps it's time to fight fire with fire one more time.

He knows the names of all the fire-children of Hawaii, the ring of five volcanoes that seethe quietly under the earth. And he also knows the name of their mother. She is awake once more. The rhythm of her breath has changed. He sighs, puts away the ukulele and opens his leather bag. It's time.

A long way away, in the soft summer darkness, the air smelled of sugar, sweat and fireworks. A fire dancer was still within a blur of light and movement. His quick hands and eyes followed and captured the flaming torches while his body stood taut and poised, relaxed on the edge of flight, as still as a hummingbird.

43

The woman sipped her drink and watched. She had been bored until now. The carnival, the dancers, the music that pulsed and throbbed, the flimsy tents with their cheap sparkling wares, were all so predictable. It was like a thousand other nights on the island. There were the tourists, plodding through the spectacle like a school of fat clumsy manatee, wooed and serviced by the smiling darting islanders. Flashing smiles, the swift pocketing of dollars as absurd little trinkets were stuffed into bloated pockets, and the endless click of cameras.

But the fire dancer was new. His beautiful face was solemn with concentration, and he seemed unaware of the cheers and applause around him. The circle of fire he spun around himself as he juggled the flaming torches enclosed him within his own world. He seemed unaware of anyone except her. His eyes caught hers just once, and there was caution and knowledge in his gaze, and recognition.

He finished his act, spread his arms wide and all his flames went out. He seemed to disappear in a wreath of smoke, but she saw his slim body twist as he stepped behind a light screen. He glanced at her again. His eyes said, 'Follow.'

The woman considered. Playing with fire is a dangerous thing. Fire warms, protects, cooks your food and comforts your cold nights, but fire has only one goal. It consumes. Did the man deserve that? She would see.

She lifted her glass to her lips. The ice had melted long ago in the warmth of her hand, and now there was a pale ghost of steam around it. Her limbs felt heavy and hot. Her long black hair coiled down to her waist in unruly curls. The alcohol had not helped, but she should know by now that it never did. She was Pele, goddess of the volcanoes, goddess of fire and lava, bringer of destruction, creator of all she surveyed, and she was so lonely that she ached. She was so lonely that she felt savage and angry as she watched the simple joys of lesser creatures around her.

To be a goddess is a cruel fate. She was here for all eternity, while smaller lives ebbed and flowed around her. They were born, they played on her beaches, swam in her tides, they loved, lived and died while she went on and on existing, forever alone. She hated them all. Her anger was rising like a jet of flame inside her, and she felt like summoning all five of her daughters to bring them to ruin in one great catastrophe of fire and molten rock.

They say that if Pele falls into despair, her anguish will be so great that the world will explode around her. All the jewel-like creatures of the water and the air will be sucked into one final tsunami, and then hurled across the universe to die in the void of space.

They say that, but they're wrong.

In the shadows, the man was waiting. His eyes glowed golden. Was it just a trick of the light? He reached out and gently took her hand. His face was hard to see, and hard to read, but she thought she saw fear there, and also pity. She was curious.

Hand in hand they walked away from the crowds along the beach. Pele listened to the waves breaking.

'I could boil the sea with a touch of my hand. It will not protect you from me,' she said.

'I know,' he replied.

They turned away from the beach and began to walk up through a grove of trees.

'This grove is tinder dry. I could consume it with a look, and I would not protect you from the flames,' she said.

'I know,' he replied again.

On and on they went together, climbing steadily higher and higher until they were above the grove. The land became steep and rocky.

'I could call lava from the rocks. You would burn to ash, and I would not protect you,' she said.

He turned towards her and took her face in his hands.

'I am not here to be protected,' he said.

He closed his eyes for a brief moment, as if to gather his courage, then he leaned forward and kissed her.

They say you can fight fire with fire. But at the end of the battle there will be nothing left but a hollow emptiness of dry heat and ashes: soundless, airless, soulless. Death and destruction with no hope of resurrection. Total annihilation.

They say that, but they're wrong.

The fire dancer and the fire goddess, wrapped in each other's arms on the warm hillside, consumed each other in a blaze of passion that lit the night and split the rock on which they lay.

But when the morning came, the beautiful man was destroyed. Her golden-eyed lover was nothing but a burned and shrivelled corpse. Pele screamed in despair when she saw what she had done, and then began to weep. Her tears flowed like a river. Clouds formed above the land and her tears rained down and down into the salty sea. Her tears washed away the dust and ashes that had been the bright and supple body and soaked the land where she lay.

Streams of Pele's tears trickled and dripped down into the secret caverns of her daughters' volcanoes and quenched the fires that burned there, until finally, utterly exhausted with grief, she fell asleep.

Her last waking thought was the final word the beautiful man had whispered in her ear before he died.

'Forget.'

And so, Pele slept, and as she slept, she healed, and forgot her despair and her anguish. She forgot her anger, and she forgot her golden-eyed lover. She sleeps still, but one day she will wake again. One day her fire will rise again, and her desire to destroy.

The old man in the yellow shirt walked slowly along the beach. The storm had passed, and the sky was washed clean. It was a beautiful tranquil day. He had left his ukulele at home and appeared to be beachcombing instead. Whatever he was looking for took a long time to find, but finally he stooped and picked up a shell. He examined it closely, chuckled with pleasure, and stowed it away in his leather bag. It might have been a trick of the light, but inside the shell there seemed to be a golden spark. If you had been able to look really carefully at the spark, you would have seen that it seemed to be a tiny golden man, curled up inside the shell, fast asleep.

They say that only gods and goddesses are immortal.

They say that, but they're wrong.

The Seagull

The seagull who came for me knew what he wanted. His instincts were sharp that day, but his method was unsure. He was a little one, still dappled-grey. The snatch-and-grab he attempted on my chips seemed vaguely desperate – a manoeuvre half-bungled, flappy and imprecise. I was hungry too, six hours into a day without breakfast, and my instincts just happened to be sharper than his. As his beak clipped the edge of my polystyrene dish and my bouquet of chips flew up into the air, I caught the bird's eye. Something primal and stupid rose up inside me. I swung for it – mindlessly, emotionlessly – like a lion swiping at a rival. A knee-jerk reaction, without thought.

I punched the seagull square in the face. Then I regained my senses.

The seagull bounced off the wall of a Harvester and broke its neck. The camera-phones already gathered around me all caught the final, twitching agonies of the bird – all except for one, who focused unwaveringly on my face. I tried to shield myself but it was far too late. My barbarity was already being uploaded, shared, captioned.

Inexplicably, people still ask me whether I've ever seen the video or not.

The small mob that chased me through the city quit halfway up Albion Hill. They were angry but unfit. I should've called somebody – the RSPB perhaps – but I was too confused and embarrassed. Instead of calling anyone, I drank Pinot Grigio until the emotions that follow a public embarrassment faded away.

I felt guilty, partly, and shaken up. My partner assured me

that though I was a bad person, we could probably put the incident behind us.

The Herald saved a spectacular action-shot of my fist squashing the victim's beak for the next morning's cover. My face, scrunched into malice by the suddenness of the violence, appeared cruel and purposeful.

I read the article in full inside the newsagents. It referred to me as the 'anonymous attacker'. A child who had seen me do it was taken to a walk-in clinic with shock. The article also urged the public for information. When I looked up from the paper, the shopkeeper lifted up a Crunchie and waved it like a gavel, telling me in a voice wobbling with emotion, 'I hope they pick you clean.'

I fled.

At home, my partner tutted as I opened two bottles of Pinot at once and drew the curtains.

The Herald found and published my name within a few days. The clear, unpixellated crest on my city council uniform had led them straight to me. My employers delivered me without a fight.

The council, from whom I thought it was impossible to get fired, fired me. The union, who had represented some of the least active and most bigoted people I'd ever worked with, refused to represent me. I went immediately onto the dole but even in the JCP the boy behind the desk wore a Sea Shepherd badge and told me there would probably be a delay with my application. He described the nature of the delay as 'unforeseen'.

People who knew me were the first to get in touch directly – former colleagues, friends. Words like 'dumbstruck', 'gobsmacked' and 'shamefaced' began to filter into my inbox. Stronger, shorter words came from strangers – words I normally wouldn't use myself but are apparently common currency among animal rights groups. Inevitably, a letter came from the RSPCA, and then from the police. Both explained that I had contravened the Wildlife and Countryside Act 1981, but whereas the police said they didn't have the resources to pursue the incident, the RSPCA threatened me with six months in jail.

The journalists appeared on my driveway and made camp. A centre-left national paper offered me a sympathetic interview and £200 in cash.

My partner told me to take it and left me with a note explaining why it would be best if we spent a little time apart and that I should definitely, under no circumstances, call.

The day I emerged from the house, my mid-morning nerves had already forced me into a breakfast of beta-blockers and Blue Nun – the last wine in the house. I came out sloppily drunk with a heart rate of fifty.

My interview with the paper was conducted in the back of a taxi, which drove repeatedly up and down the seafront past the Harvester, as if to bring up my nausea. Their questions led me to say things I wasn't sure I meant, and to omit things I'd prepared at home to help clear the air. Suddenly, everything I said seemed not to relate to the single second in which I'd punched the seagull but to gross generalisations about party-politics, the environment, even gender and race.

I was sick in the taxi. The driver swore at me in another language while he sped away, leaving me at the far end of the promenade with vomit on my trousers.

A week later a bill arrived for cleaning services. £200.

I hoped the article would be hustled into some quiet corner of the internet. Instead, it was delivered as a human-interest spread in the Sunday supplement, with a photograph of my face in high-contrast black-on-red. It explained that I was 'without remorse', that I seemed content in blaming my choices on 'Darwinian' jungle instinct, and that my reaction to the open debate around the treatment of urban wildlife was 'ambivalent to the point of psychopathy'.

By then, I was too worn down to take offence. I had already swapped white wine for Buckfast, and my ability to cry or get angry was long gone. I contemplated little and showered even less. Sitting in my house with the lights off, my soul resembled a chip that had been so trodden into the pavement even the pigeons couldn't get at it.

I called my brother-in-law and asked to speak to my partner. My brother-in-law, despite having known me for ten years, pretended he didn't know who I was, couldn't make out what I was saying, and then that he himself couldn't speak English. I should 'niet call agin'. I tried again to cry and realised I hadn't had a glass of water in several days.

My eviction notice – the product of joblessness, seclusion and drink – slid onto a tall pile of post. Since an open letter from my local MP had been published, and the Duke of York's cinema had committed to showing Jonathan Livingstone Seagull every weekend until I saw justice, the campaign against me grew wings. Twitter storms were whipped up. Blogs were churned out. Hashtags punning on my name and crime sprang up across the Internet. From outside my window, chanting woke me up in the afternoons. I heard bongos, even a DJ.

Then, an unexpected side-effect. The virulence of the campaign, allied quite clearly to certain left-leaning activist groups, brought a whole new faction to the surface – a group even more unsettling than the picket-and-placard types I grew to expect.

The countryside folk were fairly well-worded in their support of my 'cause', though I'd never indicated there should be any kind of cull, as the county gun clubs offered to facilitate. The least tolerable half of the Loose Women panel spoke of me sympathetically, and Jeremy Vine took calls from ruffled seaside traders.

Less genteel were the groups who actively worked against animal rights – groups I'd never heard of, with names like FreeTest, Furs4Fashion, the Loyalist Humanist League. Dog-kickers, probably, and people who advocated interspecies relations. Their gripes were vague and seemed to be focused more against people interested in animal welfare than against animals themselves.

Then there were the loners – deranged, misspelt messages of support from people who wanted to adopt me for crusades of their own. Meninists, neo-nationalists, disorientated radicals in varying shades. I had punched a seagull in the face, but for those men and women I had struck a blow against the secret forces of progress that threatened their daily lives.

I left their letters on the kitchen table with my keys. My partner's had been posted back long before in an unmarked envelope. I looked down at both sets and considered keeping one as a souvenir. Instead, I panicked and took the raclette, but left it on a park bench after I realised that it would probably be some time before I threw another cheese party.

The next time I saw my face in the paper I woke up cheek-to-cheek with it on the floor of a hostel. My new friends Filippa and Borek made me read it aloud to them – it mentioned the legacy of my crimes, plural – and afterwards Borek poured a can of lager over it and we got so drunk that we became best friends for about four hours. After that, Filippa found some ketamine and got caught in a loop of revolving bird-puns for far too long. I had to 'fly the coop', as she shouted several times whilst I walked away.

I still wanted to feel something, to feel anything at all, even guilt or remorse. But the cheap cider kept it all at bay. More than that, I wanted money and, if possible, human contact.

I did a job for a man whose own name was tattooed on his forearm – an unpleasant job as it turned out, though not criminal and only partly sexual. With the money I bought a two-berth tent, a camping stove and a sleeping bag. There is, however, only one place in the city where you can set up a tent for more than a week without being moved on or set on fire. So I headed to the seafront.

The air is fresh and full of salt. Now, at the brink of autumn, the sea is at its warmest. The tourist season is winding down, which means there's less noise but also less food lying around.

A fisherman gives me fish almost every day. Mackerel is

perfect for the stove. Last week a girl floated up to me with a pint in her hand and asked where I'd bought my fish and whether it'd been sustainably sourced.

Across the shingle, the seagulls totter around and occasionally laugh at me.

People still look at me disdainfully, though now it's for a different reason. Before, they were disdainful because of what I had done. Now they're disdainful because of what I no longer do – work, pay rent, wash, stay sober. They also seem angry because of the way I make them feel – guilty, a little, but more than that, afraid. They're afraid that I'll intrude, which in a cloud of super-cider and an amble across the cycle lane, I probably will.

I don't want to make people feel bad, and I want to feel something myself. Occasionally I think of my partner to try to drum up some kind of pain, but the memory is not quite strong enough. Sometimes I write poetry and recite it to people on St. James' Street. The world speeds up when I read my poetry. I don't miss work, or my house, and I definitely don't miss seeing myself on the television. But I do miss human contact.

My method for achieving this is simple. I pick a stranger, usually at night, and more often than not at the bottom of West Street. I go right up to him while he's eating his kebab – men are invariably best – and I put my face in it and just take a big bite right out of it. Then, as the doner meat slips off my chin, I meet their eye and take the full force of their fist on my face without blinking. After that, I feel the shudder and the sting as I sit back on the pavement, and I look deep inside myself and root out a feeling.

Tonight, it's apathy. Tomorrow I may do some screaming.

Don't Refuse Me

They had to break up. A new start for a new year.

Poor James, Lucy thought. She hated the fact that she would hurt him. He did love her. She felt him holding her even when they were apart.

Lucy tugged at the cellophane cover of her egg sandwich. It looked and tasted grey. Her mind puckered around the idea of what to do about James. As the train left the station, she mulled over his faults.

He doesn't want to live anywhere except London: although he can't afford it.

He doesn't like coming to visit me: he thinks Reading's boring.

Lucy had wished James into being 'the one', but he wasn't. The magic had melted, like snow turned to slush.

There was a group of teenage girls in Lucy's compartment, screeching with laughter at a video being played at full volume on someone's phone. They were drinking cider, the sharp-sweet smell filling the carriage. Lucy had been their age when she had met James. Cider was their drink then too.

She found a new, quieter seat. Then she sat with her book open on her lap, her mind returning to James.

She would start with a useless, 'I'm sorry'. He would look at her, caught between knowing and not-knowing. He would scratch his eyebrow.

'This time tomorrow…', she thought. She finished her sandwich, crushing the carton.

James' face was hidden by roses. Pinning on a smile, Lucy wondered if they were a guilt-gift. She had often hinted for him to buy flowers but usually got music by bands who James liked, from the shop in which he worked.

He works in a record shop: even though everyone buys music from Amazon.

He works 'in', when everyone else works 'for'.

She took the flowers. He kissed her. Unfamiliar, peppery aftershave wavered in the air. It mingled with a smell of roasting lamb coming from the kitchen.

'You look very smart,' she said.

James normally wore skinny jeans and T-shirts with ironic slogans. Tonight, he wore a shiny black suit. His wide pink tie was like a fat tongue.

'Happy New Year's Eve, Lucy.' James smiled, too hard. A white vein, delicate as a fishbone, throbbed at his temple. He scratched his eyebrow.

The cluttered, dusty hall felt breathless. Tinsel drooped over the banisters. Sue, a single mum of twin boys who owned the house in which James rented a room, came down the stairs. Her make up was a beige wall. She gave Lucy a one-armed hug to protect the roses.

'Don't worry, lovebirds, I'll be out of your hair soon,' Sue said. 'Sure it's still OK to put the boys to bed in an hour? They'll be no trouble for you.'

Thumps came from the floor above.

'Their dad bought them a Nintendo Switch for Christmas,' Sue said. 'James enjoys it as much as they do.'

The list was getting longer.

James took Lucy's hand and pulled her into his room. She sat on the bed, staring at the teetering towers of records. James' name tag was by her feet. She kicked it out of the way.

'I thought we'd stay in tonight,' he said.

'I thought we were going to Fish's party,' she said.

James plucked at the duvet with shaking fingers. She hoped he hadn't taken drugs. She had seen in one New Year's Eve in the A&E department of the Royal Free Hospital, while James had his stomach pumped. The whiskery old man sitting next to her had insisted on a midnight kiss.

'The party will be boring. I'm cooking for you,' he said.

'Surprise!'

'But you never cook.'

He never cooks or cleans: because he is lazy.

A flicker of annoyance crossed James' face. He pasted a smile over it.

'I love you,' he said. As the front door slammed, he trapped her in his arms.

We're so different, she thought. All we have in common is sex.

The kitchen was dimly lit by two tealights, winking between Sue's china cats. It was very hot. The rich smell of the lamb washed over her.

'This is nice, James.' A rope of fear tightened in her chest; it felt worse to dump him after he had made this effort.

'I'll get us a drink.' He was speaking very fast.

She found a vase and placed the flowers in the middle of the pine table, then she sat at it and drew circles inside faded mug rings.

James brought over two Marks & Spencer cans of gin and tonic. She downed half of hers while watching him shove bread into the toaster.

'This is lovely,' she said, quietly.

James flicked out a holly-patterned paper napkin; arranged it on her lap. A plate of pâté on toast was ceremoniously laid before her.

'Your favourite,' he said.

The toast was slathered in pâté. It filled every corner of her mouth. She saw parts of James through the roses as if he were a Picasso painting. Half a smile, half an eye.

'I wrote something for you, Lucy.' The words fizzed out of him.

James put down his barely touched toast and ran to his bedroom, bringing back his guitar.

He still thinks he's going to be a rock star: because he was in a band at school.

'Lu-cy. Do you see? What you mean to me?'

He was good at playing and singing, bad at writing lyrics. The thuds from upstairs increased like a discordant drumbeat. James' face strained with emotion. She clapped, but it wasn't the end.

When he had stopped singing, he scratched his eyebrow and looked as hopeful as a puppy wanting a walk. The tension stretched like an elastic band.

There was a scream. She ran upstairs, followed by James.

'He snatched mine off me,' Freddie wailed.

He nodded towards Benji, who was holding two game-controllers to his chest, his lips pressed into a thin line.

'I don't want to play anymore,' Benji shouted, 'and he won't let me stop.'

Lucy beckoned them over to the shabby sofa in their shared room; she made them sit each side of her. She asked them to tell her in turn what had happened, then to say sorry to each other. James stood in the doorway, can in hand. He was always surprised by how Lucy managed to calm the children. He enjoyed playing with them, but that was all. Would he be the same if he had his own kids?

He says he's too young to have children: because he still thinks he is one.

'Go and finish the dinner, James,' Lucy said gently. 'I'll put these two to bed.'

She came downstairs fifteen minutes later, having read them a story, spinning it out for longer than necessary. James was carving a rack of lamb on the hall table because a tealight had died in the kitchen.

'It looks gorgeous,' she said.

'Sue gave me the recipe.'

Again, James hardly ate. As she tried to chew, she felt his eyes on her, like heat. She had to do it - now. It was impossible to keep on chewing the dense meat, even if it did taste better than expected. She put down her fork.

'I'm sorry, James.'

'Don't worry,' James interrupted, 'I'm not that hungry

either. I'm sure we'll have room for dessert though!'

He stood to clear the plates. Sighing, she helped him. Dessert was frozen sticky toffee pudding and custard from a carton.

'James, listen….'

'Lucy….' James took a piece of paper from his trousers and peered at it in the dimness. The poem used many of the same words – maybe all of the same words – as the song. 'Lu-cy. You improve me.'

Laughter swelled inside her. As it was about to erupt, the kitchen door opened.

'I just want a drink,' Freddie said, pitifully.

She poured water into a beaker and took him back to bed, holding his hand and stroking his soft forehead; Benji was snoring gently in the top bunk. She thought what a sweet child James must have been. What a sweet child he still was.

Lucy left the kitchen door open to let in the light from the hall. James closed it, saying: 'It's more romantic in the dark, isn't it?'

'I suppose it is,' she said.

'Back to the poem,' James announced, as she sat down. 'Lu-cy. Don't refuse me.'

A cold fear was forming inside Lucy. In the semi-darkness, the fridge freezer glared. She jumped as James' foot rubbed her shin.

'James,' she said, when he had finished. She said it to his back; he was opening a bottle of champagne. 'James.' The word was like the last puff of air leaving a balloon. She tried to pull herself together.

The cork exploded.

'Tell me in a minute, baby. I've got something for you.'

He pulled a carrier bag from under the table.

The big box had been gift-wrapped. There was a teddy bear inside, wearing a leather waistcoat and holding a fabric guitar; a felt heart was on one of its arms.

'Press the heart,' James said excitedly.

58

She pressed.

'I love you,' the bear said, in James' voice. 'Will you marry me?'

The front door crashed open, followed by the kitchen door. The light from the hall was blinding. Sue stood there, red-faced, carrying two bottles of prosecco. Three women teetered behind her.

'You did it!' Sue cried to James; to Lucy, she said: 'Wasn't the bear a brilliant idea? Congratulations, both of you!'

'Congratulations,' echoed the friends.

The Snowman

This marvellous snow. He scoops huge handfuls up as he walks down the road. It sits in willing piles on top of stone walls and iron gates, on the squat bushes and smug little hedges that populate this part of town, this self-satisfied place he used to call home. His breath appears in white furls. He feels like a dragon that has been temporarily extinguished. How much more would he prefer to be breathing flames, not smoke. Global warming? Global freezing more like. He slaps his wet hands together. Drops fly up into his face.

Once upon a time he had gloves. She kept them in a bin-bag under the stairs, all the hats, scarves and gloves together, ready for winter. There were hundreds; she said they bred in the dark. He used never to be short of a bit of winter warmth.

Cars drive slowly past, afraid of the mounting snow. He glances sideways at drivers and passengers, warm and enclosed behind glass and steel. He scoops up more snow and balls it then flings it over a wall. A woman driver catches his eye then looks away. What you looking at, he thinks. Or has he said it out loud? Is he talking to himself again?

His feet make a prolonged sound each time he takes a step, crunching followed by sucking followed by scraping, as he meets soft snow, buried compacted snow, then slush. Every step is an effort, and he is wearing the wrong shoes. Of course, it should be wellington boots in this weather, but they were under the stairs too, so he has on an old pair of walking boots. The snow is deep and creeps over the tops. She must have enough winter accessories to open a shop, and most of them are his.

He remembers when she first told him. Sat in the garden, it was sunny, he was in shirt sleeves, the kids were playing on the trampoline and she said, 'You must see it's got to that point now; we can't go back.' At first, he thought she was referring to the over-long grass or the ill-fated extension; these were the usual topics of conversation for a Sunday afternoon. But her expression told him differently. Maybe he did know, but he wouldn't admit it. Weeks of argument ensued – hers, calm and reasonable as though there couldn't be any dispute – his, violent, spluttering, spitting his words out, waking in the night gripped by panic, a sense of disappearing down a black hole of his own making, imploding into himself, walking in the dark, even in daylight hours.

Then she became angry too. Nothing was changing, he wasn't accepting the inevitable; they were still living under the same roof. This was the root of the problem, wasn't it? He had never changed. Oh yes, he'd promised change, promised a career not a job, new friends, new opportunities, a more hopeful, brightly lit outlook. He needed to get that they were a successful couple and start acting like it, shake off his provincial grim-up-north attitude. She actually said that, and then laughed ruefully at her own cleverness. She always had a good turn of phrase. This was partly what had attracted him to her, her sharp wit, her way with words. And her red hair and bright blue eyes and her crooked toothy smile and her soft mouth and her plump hands and her freckled back and her voice when she said, I love the way you look at me like that.

He presses more snow between his bare hands and aims it at a leafless tree. Snow falls from bare branches down the back of his bare neck. There are droplets on his cheeks, in his eyes, round his numb lips and his ears. Never have so many small parts of him felt so unsafe, so unprotected. So now he is that man who has left his home, and who comes back at weekends to collect his children. Now he walks from the small flat to this smart, self-satisfied neighbourhood which had once been his, but where, she was right, he never felt he had belonged. She has made new friends, joined the book club, bought organic, and has her hair cut into a shiny bob.

A car horn sounds. He looks up. Three youths lean out of the window, jeering and pointing. 'Alright mate, how you doing mate, nice and cold are you?' They sound the horn again. He reddens under his clothing, he must have drawn attention to himself, and he must have been talking out loud this time. It has to stop. He has to get a grip before reaching the house or the kids will realise, and they won't want to go with him. It had nearly got to that point last week, Cassie reluctantly buttoning up her jacket in the hallway, Aidan taking ages to find some damn stupid car or train he said he couldn't be without. It was obvious they didn't want to come.

Snow seems to be soaking into his underclothes now, or maybe it is sweat. He is hot under this coat, this ill-fitting coat he had retrieved in his unseemly panic to leave. It had come to a head one day; she had threatened to put his stuff out on the pavement like in a soap opera and talked ominously about police and restraining orders and his growing unpredictable temper. He said, was it any wonder? She was killing him. Then he became aware of Cassie standing at the bottom of the stairs with a look on her face he would never forget. She was terrified of him. She saw him as he really was - a mad man, a misfit, spewing out anger and foul words she'd probably never even heard before, certainly not with the no-TV-after-7-o'clock rule.

He stops and kicks the toe of each boot, viciously, against a stone wall. Snow off leather. He kicks again, so hard this time that his toes hurt. More cars pass, wipers flailing. He feels eyes upon him, maybe people he'd once stood next to in the school playground. What must he look like, ill-dressed against the cold, walking back to his ex-home, ranting to himself, slowly disappearing under muffling snow? He walks under a low hanging tree, reaches up and snaps a branch with his bare hands. He walks on, using the branch first of all as a makeshift walking stick, then as a sword, slicing through the air, beating back the snowflakes, and then as a baton, tossing it into the air, catching it, trying to twirl it. Cassie does this, majorettes, clever girl, it's harder than it looks. He is whistling tunelessly, the notes rising from his lips, the stick flying through the air, landing in his hand, flying through the air again.

He is nearly at the house. He can see from the bottom of the street, Steven's shiny new Audi parked outside his gate. It's Steven, Daddy, not Steve. Mummy says we have to call him Steven. He is startled by someone saying his name. Alright, Tom, how are you? It's his old neighbour. The figure passes before he can reply. He is flooded once again with a sense of shame so strong, it was like a wet rag wrung over him. He pushes the tip of the branch through the snow, his breathing noisy, mounting the hill to his old house. He almost doesn't recognise it, the garden, roof and gateposts adorned ice cream cone white.

There is something on the grass. He walks up to it. For a second in the dazzling winter sun he almost thinks it might be human, but of course it's not. They have built a snowman. It is tall and fat and solid. It wears a hat, his hat, jauntily placed. It has a carrot nose, like in a children's story, and pebble eyes. Its mouth is a crescent shaped indent smiling cheerily. He drops his gaze. At its base a name has been picked out in small stones. Steven. They've named it.

The snowman's head separates from its body with sudden, vigorous excitement. Its nose and eyes are sent in various directions. Snow rises up and a thud is heard as it sails across the lawn. He watches his hands. He is holding the stick. He has done it. This marvellous snow! He rains down more and more blows on the body. At first it resists but then it yields, collapsing and exploding, losing its human aspect. He is stamping it down with his feet. The stick has snapped in two. There are hot tears on his face. He is appalled. He looks up. A noise like a sob and a groan escapes from his mouth.

Daddy. She has come out of the house and is walking towards him. His insides turn to water. He could die here now in the snow, please let it happen. His daughter has seen him. Daddy what's wrong? She takes the remainder of the stick from his hand and lays it quite gently on the ground. 'You're cold.

Please come in and get warm.' Her voice is kind; her expression is anguished. She holds out her hand. He takes it. They start to walk towards the house.

The Egg and the Skipping Rope

I opened my first art gallery when I was seven years old. Mr. Holloway told me the best artists named their gallery after the street they lived on, so I named mine Galerie Rue Saint-Jacques. It opened once a week, on Saturday mornings, when I knew my best patron Matthew Holloway would be passing by on his way back from the village, carrying fresh baguettes that looked like biros in his enormous hands.

He was the tallest man I knew, and his head was the only one that I ever saw reach above the front hedge. His steps were so big that his head would come in and out of view, as though someone was bouncing a large rubber egg off the footpath on the other side. When I saw the egg bouncing towards the village, I'd message in on a radio made from my hand and say: 'Shh, the egg is in the village. Repeat. The egg is in the village.' Then I'd hurry inside and get my art ready for display.

Northern France always seemed to have good weather, especially on Saturdays, so I set my paintings up on the patio behind our red brick house. There was a piece cracked off the patio with a small cavity behind it, and one day I pulled it away and there was a big rat inside. I stood there frozen. I didn't know what to do, so I just put the piece of concrete back in its place. My mam said it was a possum when I described it to her, because it had a long thin snout but I told everyone it was a rat anyway.

When her friends came over, I'd say, 'Be careful where you sit. There's a rat in the garden.'

'That wasn't a rat,' my mother would say back, 'it was a possum.'

'It was a rat. A big fat one too.'

One of my paintings on display was of a great big shining sun that was so big I had to draw it as an oval so that it would fit on the page. It was inspired by a stand-off I'd had with my teacher Monsieur Desén. We fell out over the weather.

Every day in school, someone different was picked to draw the weather on a special chart in the corner of the classroom. Whoever was picked, was given the website www.meteofrance.fr and instructions on a piece of paper on how to look it up.

The row had happened on a nice day. The sky was blue, with just a few specks of cloud, and it was warm enough that some teachers were even teaching their classes outside. I was picked, and I drew a sun so huge it had to be drawn as an oval to fit on the whiteboard.

'T'as pas oublié quelque chose?'

Did you forget something?

'Non.'

'T'es sûr?'

'Oui.'

Monsieur Desén then pushed down on his hairy arms and lifted himself from behind his desk and erased the sun from the weather chart. He explained that we had some cloud today and asked could I redraw the picture.

I drew a full sun again.

He looked straight at me and wiped the board clear for the second time. He said I had to draw the clouds because it was a cloudy day.

I was getting cross. I made these big, puffy breaths as though I was trying to inflate myself up to his size. 'D'accord,' I said. But instead of picking up the whiteboard marker, I picked up the permanent marker we used to name our art folders, and I drew the big oval sun again, with rays of sunlight coming off it in all directions.

'It's a perfect day, and you don't even know it!' I screamed at him.

I started crying, and the school rang home. Mam could

speak French, and she went to the school to hear the good news. Dad couldn't, and he went to the school to ignore the bad. Monsieur Desén tersely handed me over to my dad.

This was my first painting for viewing, and it was called Monsieur Desén's Favourite Weather.

'Shh, the egg is coming back, the egg is coming.' I got my position ready and stood by my paintings with my arms folded behind my back. The lock on the wooden gate in the hedgerow clinked open, and in came Matthew Holloway.

'Bonjour Monsieur,' I bowed.

My mam would come out then and they'd say hi and do cheek-kisses even though neither of them were French. Then she'd take his bread inside and prepare fresh coffee while he examined my paintings.

He'd muse aloud while he leaned down to inspect them.

'Hmm…sunny,' he said, looking at Monsieur Desén's Favourite Weather, 'Lucy did say she was looking for ways to brighten up the kitchen.' I'd listen to every word and look for clues as to which one he'd buy.

On he went to the next painting, which was of a bag of flour with roses sticking out of it. 'I do love to bake, but I'm not sure how pleased Lucy would be to find thorns in her sponge cake…'

'I better go discuss the options with your father,' and with that he'd head down the patio to the decking chairs and sit and chat with my father, the coffee ready, and the patisserie he brought with him plated and cut into slivers on the table.

Then came the Great Wait. After hassling Mam in the kitchen, I'd go upstairs to my parents' room and open the window slightly. Then I'd lie down on the beige carpet and listen to my father and Matthew talking down below. I learnt lots of stuff through that window. I knew about Tony Blair and Jacque Chirac. I didn't know who the IRA were, but I learnt the word 'ceasefire'. Shania Twain, tumours, Oasis, boob jobs.

My ears pricked when I heard my dad tell him about the

phone call from Monsieur Desén, which my sister had to translate, and the two of them, thinking that no one was listening, let out big laughs.

Matthew said, 'I am surprised he didn't scrub it off with that big moustache of his.'

I was rolling around laughing at that one.

I could tell when he was about to leave because there would be a slight pause in the conversation, and then Matthew would say, 'I better get back to Lucy.'

Lucy was the only woman I knew who had pigtails. She was tall too, not tall enough for her head to be seen over the hedge, but tall enough that her pigtails would bounce up and down into view. And when the two of them walked by the house together, they became The Egg and the Skipping Rope.

Matthew bought Monsieur Desén's Favourite Weather for ten francs that day, then the lock on the gate clinked, and the egg bounced home.

Mam started going to the Holloways' house to help Lucy. Lucy had never needed help before, so I asked my mam what she was doing over there. 'Making sandwiches,' she said. One of the days I went with her to the Holloways' because there was no one at home to mind me. We stopped in Shopi to buy bread.

I guarded the trolley while she went into the vegetable aisle for salads. I didn't want to see cauliflowers. Mam had sat with me on the stairs to explain it. 'It can come in two ways. Some are shaped like a golf ball, and some like a cauliflower. Matthew's is like a cauliflower so they can remove the big bit, but they're not able to remove all the small bits. And the small bits can grow back.'

After lunch, Lucy and my mam went into the garden to sunbathe because it was a nice day. Lucy had poured me a glass of apple juice with a straw in it and asked if I'd bring it in to Matthew. The Holloways' hallway was big and open with white tiles, and the TV room was in an alcove just off it. I stopped around the corner from the alcove and stood against the wall. I could hear French cartoons, and there was a breeze.

When I went in, Matthew was sitting on the couch. He was all puffy like the Michelin Man. He didn't look fat, but as if someone had used a pump and pumped him up. His skin was shiny, and a fan was blowing air at him. His eyes moved and he saw me, but his head stayed still.

I went to put the juice down and the TV remote fell off the coffee table. The cartoon switched over to nine mini-screens with blue channel listings down the side. Matthew started making groaning noises.

They had gotten a big satellite dish and they had 399 channels. There were two remotes, and they sometimes needed to be used together. I tried to change it back, and the channel changed to a blur of black and white and made a fuzzing noise. Matthew started making loud 'ughhhh' sounds. I didn't know what to do so I ran away, and Matthew was left stuck there looking at a wall of black and white.

Lucy found me in the utility room. 'He's turning into the Michelin Man,' I cried.

Dad started reading the Sunday paper up at the Holloways', and unlike Mam and the sandwiches, I knew what he was doing. When he came home, I would lie on the floor in the front room with my eyes closed, and Dad would describe what was going on up there.

'So I had a coffee in the alcove, and Matthew had his apple juice...I read him out the news that Tony Blair got in – he enjoyed that one...then he starting having a snooze, so I turned on the Street Sharks before I left because I know he'll like that on when he wakes up.'

He took a small parcel out of his pocket and handed it down to me.

'I was also given this,' he said.

I opened the brown parcel, and inside was a paintbrush and

69

a note written in big difficult writing: 'Where is le petit artiste?'

'Looks like you're being commissioned,' said Dad with a wink.

I had a painting I'd been preparing in secret for Matthew, for the next time he came to visit Galerie Rue Saint-Jacques. Mam wanted to check it before we brought it over, to make sure it was suitable, but I said if anyone looks at it before Matthew I'd scream. I kept it wrapped in a beach towel on my lap in the car.

When we got there Lucy had the alcove ready, and Matthew looked like he was on holiday because he was wearing a Hawaiian shirt and there was an umbrella in his apple juice.

I set the painting up on the coffee table and pulled the towel off. Lucy and Mam both said that it was lovely straight away, but I knew they didn't know what it was. 'Is it Monsieur Desén's Favourite…Sunset?'

The bottom half of the page was all green. Above the green poked a big egg. And going over the top of the egg was a yellow rope.

Matthew made a noise, and when Lucy leaned in to hear him, he lifted his finger and flicked one of her pigtails. I started laughing, and Matthew made more noises, which I knew was him laughing. Lucy and my mam started laughing too, although I knew they still didn't get it. It was only me and Matthew who knew what was going on. It was only Matthew who found my art funny, and that's why he will always be my greatest patron.

Through the Window

If I asked you to describe what a property in London looks like, you'd probably describe a pristine white Victorian terrace, complete with a Juliet balcony. Maybe some climbers would form a perfect, flowered archway over the door.

But I, like most in London, live in an apartment. Pretty much the same as an apartment anywhere in the world, I imagine. I can't be sure though; I've never stayed in an apartment in any other city. It was straight from my parents' place in the suburbs, to halls at university, to this apartment, when I landed my first job in a communications agency. Just to be thorough, and in case my experience is vastly different from any of yours, my apartment is part of a 12-storey complex in the heart of south London; it's hugged on each side by complexes of similar sizes and is sound-tracked by the overground which is a few hundred metres away. The walls and ceilings are thin enough to hear the sound of kids jumping on floorboards in the morning, and parents having arguments and/or sex at night. Each building is surrounded by a moat of overflowing garbage bins stuffed with the remains of Ubereats.

I could walk, reach, lean, over all 273 square feet of this place half-asleep. It feels like home though, in the kind of way that when my friends used to come over, they would comment, 'Ah, smells just like your place always smells, Ilona.' I guess when you've endowed your apartment with its own signature scent that probably means you've settled right in. I wonder if that scent has changed now, after being practically homebound for the last eight months, without the floral hints of loved friends and mixed spirits?

Just after lunch, as I tidy the pillows on the couch to set myself up there for an afternoon of Netflix and work, I look through the window and into the apartment complex opposite me. There are only three apartments I can see directly into properly, each one stacked on top of the other. The top one has a television against the window (a travesty to waste the scarce natural light in London, if you ask me), and the bottom always has its curtains drawn. I haven't paid enough attention to see whether there is any light from beneath the curtains at night, but maybe I will. The apartment in the middle has a girl in it. It seems to be just her living there. Well, all I can see is her living space and kitchen, but I imagine if someone else were to live there, I probably would have seen them in the last few months of increasingly frequent glances across.

The girl is standing, leaning over her kitchen island which she has converted into a workspace. She alternates between hacking at her keyboard and slurping at the cup of noodles on the table. Over the last few weeks, I've seen the gradual expansion of her standing desk: first she got a stand, then the keyboard mat, then the little dock for her phone. Marvelling at her as she works, I can't help feeling like I have been a silent witness to it all, providing silent and unheard cheerleading support from my apartment to hers.

I settle onto the couch and open Netflix: Episode 1 of *The Queen's Gambit*. Netflix has this feature where, whenever you open the website, it immediately begins playing the first episode of their promoted 'headline' show. I've seen the same 30 seconds of *The Queen's Gambit* so many times I feel like I might as well just watch it now.

Waking up and walking with my eyes half open to the bathroom, I realise that it has been two years to the month since I moved into this apartment. Two years since filter-searching for apartments within a 5-mile radius of my work and under a 1000 pounds a month; there were a handful of options, and this one was the only one with a window larger than my head. A match made in heaven.

It feels like, in the last two months especially, I have been talking to myself a lot more. Have you found that?

As I begin preparing breakfast, I notice that the girl isn't at her standing desk but at the couch. This is the first weekday morning in weeks I haven't seen her working as I make my oats. She seems to start work just as I get up. I have no idea what she does, but I'm convinced that it is more important than what I do given the wealth of evidence before me. No, today, she is strewn across the couch, watching none other than *The Queen's Gambit*. Having binged the first three episodes only last night, I know exactly where she is up to in the second episode.

Already on the second episode. I smile to myself.

She points at the TV, then at me, nodding as she puts her thumb up. She animates her movements to make sure her mime is as clear as possible.

I do my best attempt at a curtsy. No worries, happy to recommend television shows any time.

Of course, I do see friends for 'exercise' in the park every week or two, but walking through a semi-deserted London for two hours, seeing nothing but closed shopfronts, it feels artificial. At least, I find myself unable to really be there in those moments. All I can think about is how many hands touched the lights at the pedestrian crossing before mine, and constantly make myself mental reminders to always wear my woolly gloves outside and take hand-sanitiser with me.

Family, you ask, the ones from the suburbs? Well, Dad is getting chemotherapy, so we decided it would be best if I stayed put until this whole thing blew over. We had that conversation around April or May this year, before we realised that this was more than a passing wind. We haven't revisited the conversation since. Every time I thought to bring it up, I've bit my tongue.

I notice that she is playing chess online. I think I read somewhere that chess.com had something like a 200% spike in people on their website in the weeks after the show. Crazy how one show can become such a global phenomenon, isn't it? I'd like to think I was an OG-Original (chess) Grandmaster; I used to play in high school when only the coolest of the cool kids would give up their Friday afternoons to play.

More than anything else, my days lack rhythm. Before, I would be getting ready until 8am, commuting until I was sat at my desk at 8.30pm, working until 5.30pm, then back home or to a friend's or to drinks after work from 6pm. Now, I wake up around 7.30am, and by the time I'm sitting on the toilet scrolling through my phone, there are already work emails firing at me. With everyone working from home, without the commute, they just expect us to be on call at all times. The whole day goes like this, shuffling mindlessly through 273 square feet of thick fog.

I called my parents yesterday, asked them what their plans were for Christmas. It's only a fortnight away. Mum said she was just on her computer, putting items in her Waitrose basket. It's a marvel, she said, shopping from home. It all comes direct to your door, the same day. I thought about asking whether I should come home or not, but I didn't bother. Dad was too tired to talk, but I told him I loved him, and he said he loved me too.

Mum said it's his last cycle of chemotherapy, then hopefully, fingers crossed, the cancer will be in remission. Six months, Mum said, over and over, six months, until they can definitely tell us whether it's in remission. And I'm sure this will all blow over by then. You'll be back home and in your swimmers for summer. Absolutely no time at all.

The standing desk is completely de-assembled; the girl seems to have committed to a career in amateur chess (that, or she has time off over Christmas, but I prefer my theory). I think about making an account myself. Who knows, maybe we will end up playing a game against each other - imagine the odds of that!

Walking over to the wall where my whiteboard is, I try and rub out the to-do list from 23rd November. The ink has set into the board as if tucked into the whiteboard out of weariness. Scrubbing it ferociously like the bottom of a burnt pan, I pause for a moment, before writing in big caps:

Want to play a game of chess?

I hold it up against the window of the apartment. I realise I could be standing here for an hour or even more until the girl looks over and decide that ten minutes will be my time limit. And so I stand at the window, twisting my neck in increasingly more frequent intervals to see when I can end this embarrassment. After about 7 minutes, she looks at the board. She stands in front of her window and nods. She fetches a piece of A3 paper and comes to the window and then puts her finger up.

She jogs out of my view of her living room and returns with a thick marker:

SURE. HOW DO WE DO IT?

KNIGHT B5
King C2
QUEEN E7
Checkmate?

Her face is a cocktail of hesitation and excitement. We have been playing a few games for the last week or so, and this is her first victory. Each from our own living rooms, I have set up my chess board with two chairs on either side of the table, alternating between sides depending on whose turn it is. She just leans over and moves my pieces for me, but I get a kick out of pretending to be both her and me. When I'm acting like her, I look up and scratch my chin, tapping it occasionally, just like she does.

Good game! Another?

She shrugs her shoulders happily in response - why not? It's the 20th of December now, and apparently the prime minister is going to hold an address to the country at 4pm. Still a few hours and games of chess to be played before then!

I set up the board again; it's my turn to be white, so I move my pawn and then walk over to the window:

Pawn E4

GOING HOME BEFORE THE RESTRICTIONS
MERRY XMAS
LOVE, TALIA X

Talia. Does she look like a Talia? What does that even mean anyway?

Makes sense, though. Boris just announced Tier 4 yesterday, banning travel outside of your local area from midnight. It's morning now, and her curtains are drawn for the first time in weeks, her hand-written message on the window is all that's left.

I make myself a cup of tea. I sit on the couch and turn on the TV. The marathon of Christmas movies has begun. The room feels a bit cold, so I swathe myself in a blanket and settle in for the festive season.

Cocoa Tea

Some people don't know they are blessed. Manny Thomas never had that problem – his mother reminded him daily.

'What for you crying, Manny? Don't you know we born on the most wonderful island in God's creation?'

Born and raised in a small tin shack on the edge of Dominica, Manny counted his blessings every day.

First, there was his firm but fair mama with her all-enveloping hug, a sharp quote from the Gospels and good honest cooking. On a Friday, Johnny cakes and fish fry, roast meat on a Sunday after church and, if you were lucky, spiced buns on Saturday afternoon.

Then there was his father. Rarely around as he travelled the island in his battered old jeep, going about his business. Mama had explained how lucky they were to have 'a gentleman' as master of the house. 'Well, you know, he never beat me, he never fight, he never go out with other women, don't drink, and he brush up for the church like a good honest Christian.'

Manny only had to look at the fathers of his friends to see that these were unusual qualifications. But what he liked most was that his dada always brought something back from his trips – sweet lemongrass, ripe mangos or coconuts. Sometimes, he brought the weird looking 'devil's apple' which his mother wouldn't touch but which he and his father hacked apart with their machetes, enjoying the sweet pulp in silent complicity.

And there was this welcoming world of the island where snakes and spiders posed no threat. His mama said it was the Garden of Eden and that one could survive simply by picking fruit from trees in the forest. Of course, there was fruit he'd been warned to avoid at the threat of death, but one could still venture out in only a T-shirt and shorts, swim in the white river, climb up to the volcanic mountains and hot lakes and explore the world to his heart's content.

Finally, there was his mama's cocoa tea. The ultimate and perpetual balm for all ills. If he scraped his knee, there was cocoa tea. When angry guard dogs scared him as he climbed the fence of the soap factory, cocoa tea. When the skies grew black and they cuddled inside their flimsy home, scared witless by the threat of the hurricane, somehow Mama still managed to conjure up thick, creamy, chocolatey cocoa tea on their little paraffin stove.

As he grew older, he began to look for other boys and girls his age for company, and the cocoa tea was still in ready supply for soothing heartbreaks and disappointments. 'Plenty more fish in the sea,' she would say.

Somehow, though, he changed. It was around the time he discovered ganja, started smoking the weed, searching out the dark and desperate music from Jamaica. 'What, you think you're a Rasta, boy?' she would shout in frustration.

It was at this time his father became weak. Returning late one night from a party, Manny found his father groaning softly. Mama held him with one arm while feeding him sips of cocoa tea. He had tried to effect nonchalance, but his view of the world was somehow shattered.

'It up to you now, boy. You gotta work, and the good Lord will provide.'

His dad's health got worse, and soon he lapsed into a pathetic state, bed-ridden and without appetite.

So, Manny took his father's old jeep and began his rounds – picking up supplies and doing odd jobs for many small guesthouses around the island. But his heart wasn't in it; all he wanted was to hang out with friends. He became unreliable, missing appointments and disappearing halfway through jobs. His shoddy work saw him sacked, time after time, from the service of different establishments. He could see it coming in people's eyes. They would sigh and tell him how much they had admired his father, how sorry they were, but…

He became contemptuous of his clients and, soon enough, one or two of his customers noticed that small, cashable items were missing. The showdown came one Sunday after his mother had been to church. Word had got around that her son was now considered a 'scoundrel child' and not fit to be part of the community.

When he turned up for Sunday dinner, instead of roast on the table and cocoa tea on the stove, he found a note. It said, 'This is a house of God and you are no longer welcome here – take your things and go. Don't come back until you are right in the head. Remember – time like a scorpion, sting without warning.'

He sat back heavily on the stool with a new type of buzzing in his forehead. Then, mechanically, he filled his bag with his few precious belongings. He paused by the stove and reached for the jar filled with raw cocoa sticks. Outside the house he was suddenly wracked with sobs. Hardly able to see through his tears, he got into his father's truck and took off across the island.

Three weeks later, his father died.

Manny lived in his truck for six months, taking advantage of all the nature the island had to offer: swimming and washing in the sea and the rivers, taking food where he found it – in the wild, or from a farmer's field. Taking diesel too, skilfully draining various generators. He drifted away from his former gang, for whom he seemed just a little too wild, a bit too scary, with his hair now matted, thick and long. From time to time, he stole or worked for a bottle of rum or a bag of weed, but these tastes left him too. Eventually, he spent his nights on deserted roads, staring up at the millions of stars above him.

He was roaming across the wild, unclaimed land high in the mountains when he got his wake-up call. Normally he was careful to avoid other people, but today he was distracted by the sun on his face and the smell of the land after a rainfall. He suddenly came face-to-face with Big Sam, one of his father's best friends.

'Manny! That you, son?'

He grunted his assent, too surprised to brush past as he would have liked to have done.

'I can hardly see you through all the hair, boy. But listen up good. Your mama is real bad.' He reached out a strong hand to Manny, who flinched but then allowed him to grip his forearm. 'You need to get to her – as soon as you can.'

The message was clear, and although it recreated the familiar buzzing in his head, Manny was off. He crashed through the undergrowth and in forty minutes he was at the truck. He gunned the engine and set off.

His mama was lying on the makeshift couch, surrounded by a gaggle of brightly dressed ladies, many of whom crossed themselves or muttered prayers when Manny's hairy form filled the bright doorway.

'Leave me now, ladies. God bless, I'm going to talk to my son.' The crowd dispersed slowly, like a flutter of butterflies. 'Come to me, Manny.'

He knelt by his mama's side, cautiously taking the proffered hand. She looked him up and down. 'How you doing, boy?'

He hadn't spoken a word to another human being in five weeks. 'Umm…' he licked his dried lips. 'I'm ok, I guess.'

'Manny?'

'Yes?'

'Will you make me some cocoa tea?'

'Oh… ah, yes.' He stumbled to his feet and went to the stove. He pulled down the heavy-bottomed pan and put in a tin of coconut milk. He looked around for cocoa sticks.

'Don't you remember?' his mama said weakly. 'You took them when you left.'

He was seized with urgency and ran to the van. He scrabbled around until, amazed, he rooted out the clear glass jar with the cocoa sticks still inside. Racing back into the house, he grated and added the cocoa, along with cane sugar, nutmeg, cinnamon, and just a touch of bay leaf. The concoction quickly warmed up over the paraffin.

'Come and sit by me, child. We'll watch the stove together.'

He sat down, and his mother put her arm around him. She let out a painful, rasping cough. 'Now, I don't know what happen with you, child. But I know that the Lord is willing to give you another chance.' He seized on this with desperation.

'Do you really think so, Mama?'

'I think so. Now go and fetch the tea.' He went over to the stove and filled two tin mugs with the precious liquid.

His mother took a long sip. 'Aah. Your mama taught you well.' She cackled, then dissolved into another fit of vicious coughing.

The taste of cocoa brought back in an instant every bit of love that had been poured into him. His father's gifts of exotic fruit and flowers, his mother's cooking and constant care. His body began to shake with pent-up tears, and he bowed his head into his mother's lap, all the pain and confusion and sorrow pouring out.

'There, there, Manny. Everything will be alright. Don't you know you're blessed, Manny? We're both blessed.' And, with her son in her arms and cocoa tea in her hand, she closed her eyes to sleep.

Little Hell

He has been to the end of the earth and back.

Now he is standing ten feet from his house and there is his son, crouching down low, picking something up, a stone or a piece of rubble. Any moment he will raise his small, filthy head and see him, and together they will have to navigate this moment, which feels as perilous as when the boat was carrying him away across the wide, blank sea.

The boy's face is less round, as if it has been rubbed away by an invisible hand. The same hand has stretched him out, so his legs are two long, thin sticks with bulges at the knees. His face is dirty, almost black in parts and then in others it is a translucent white. His knitted smock is unravelling at the sleeve. He, Huw, takes all this in, in one second, one heartbeat. They are suspended, the two of them, as though time is running the opposite way that it should, the last three years gone by in a rush and now this tiny moment stretched out like an elastic band before it goes slack.

His son looks up. His face is blank. And then he calls out, 'Mam', and again, 'Mam. Mae dyn yma.' Not da then. Just a man. And then there is Gwyn at the door, thinner too, and he knows that she has seen him and that in the same slow split second she has seen his shoes, held together with string, the ragged ends of his trousers splattered with mud and horseshit from the road, the hunted look of him. And she knows.

He walks towards her, as he cannot very well walk anywhere else, and they wrap their two pairs of thin arms around him awkwardly and around the big bag on his back. He sees her eye it hopefully, just for a moment, but then without having to ask or speak at all she looks away, for what man makes his fortune in gold then walks the seven hours home from Swansea with his shoes flapping in two pieces.

She turns and walks in, out of the stench of the narrow passage between the houses where a child is pissing, and he follows her inside. He sees the shape of the chairs, the stove, the familiar wrinkle of their bed. He stoops under the low ceiling and places his bag down to the floor with a thump.

His son is chattering now, a bullet spray of questions, about Australia, what it is like, about what trains he rode, and about what creatures he saw, and he sees that Gwyn has told the boy stories and that some of them are real and that some are as fantastical as fairy tales. And he sees the distance between himself and Gwyneth is not any smaller now than it had been when he had been on the other side of the world. He is the only one who knows, who will ever know, what the reality is of that place, what the scope is of the world. A great wave of something washes over him, a feeling so strong that for a second, he thinks he might vomit, and he realises that it is homesickness. He is nauseous with longing for his tent on the edge of the Ballarat river, his brother David, for the flags on every corner, the brawls and gunshots at night and the music, the accordions and fiddles and guitars all playing their own, clashing song at a hundred thousand fires across the squalid camp. For the heat and brightness and the sun scorching his head and arms. He wonders if he is the first man ever to walk into his own home and become instantly homesick.

His wife looks at him again, weighing him up. Instinctively she reaches out and touches him on the arm where the sun has burned it a dark leathery red, as if she can't quite believe it is him, or perhaps it is only that she can't believe that a person could be such a colour, and then pulls away again and turns to put the water over the stove.

He stands there, watching his small, tough wife lit by the glow of the stove, and an image comes unbidden, unwanted into his head, of a girl in Ballarat, an obscene thought. He pushes it down so hard his head gives an involuntarily shake and his son, who is loitering now in the doorway, looks at him, wary.

His brother had not wanted to come home to this hell pit, and had no one to come home for, his family all dead from the sickness five years ago. Characters from a distant drama now. But he, Huw, has these two thin strangers, and so here he is, back in this place so dark and grey that it is as if they are living inside the rock rather than on top of it. 'We are men of the earth, Huw,' his father used to say. But his father had been a farmer, so his earth was living and fertile, close to the air and the sky and things that breathe. Not the grit and the static depths of Merthyr, with its people all working day after day, burrowing down towards hell. His life is metal, not soil, he thinks; he follows it like a magnet, first to his house standing here on the iron slag heap, then drawn to the gold and pulled back across the world to the iron again. 'For God's sake, stay,' David had said. 'There's nothing for any of us there. It's a little fucking hell.' But they had both known he was powerless in the pull of it.

They have still not said a word, he and his wife. She straightens up from the stove and stands with her arms folded, her expression unfathomable. Her shoulders hunch in a way they didn't use to, as though his failure sits perched on them. Huw reaches into his pocket and takes out the small parcel of handkerchief and string that he has carried halfway across the world. He unfolds it while she watches him, and there they are, the two flashes of gold lying on the cotton. Two little earrings. He stands there with his hand outstretched, offering the handkerchief and its contents.

It is all he has to show for his three years; the sum total of his little yield which had flowed from the claim next to his, because his own claim was a dud, and went down to the riverbed without touching the seam of gold. So for months he had worked, knee deep in the mud, sifting and panning with the heat beating down on his head, his hands by turns like puffed white sea creatures in the water then stiff and cracked at night, splitting down their seams when he bent his fingers. And only these crumbs of gold had glinted in his pan, each one bringing a second of euphoria, of hope, of a kind that he had never known. But instead of the luck of the Irish, he has the luck of the Welsh. If he had known that in the end it would be a game of luck, all this, like the games he played when he was a kiddie, which way will the stone land or flip a coin, he would not have taken the boat.

It was David who had come back from Swansea with the newspaper. They had looked at it, he and his wife, at the great colour picture on the front page with the man looking out to sea, and at the words beneath, at the promises made. They had sat with it and talked into the night, and the colour had rubbed off on his hands, not just the black of the ink, but the vermilion and rose and vivid blue of the Australian sky. They had decided. He would set off with David and leave Gwyn and his son to the care of their eldest brother. And he knew even then, before the adventure had even begun, that the payment he would have to make for this miraculous escape would be the moment of return.

She looks at the earrings, his wife, then nods, tightly, and he sees there are hot tears in her eyes. Gwyn doesn't cry, not even for their dead children, for her dead mother. Not from hunger, from pain or childbirth. She is as hard as the rock they are standing on. He wants to say that he is sorry, that he has brought the earrings as a gift because of how sorry he is, but he can't make his mouth form the lie. He has brought his gold home for himself, because he could not give it up. Before leaving Ballarat, he had taken his tiny collection of nuggets, painstakingly kept, to the smithy's, and there he had had them fashioned into these two plain earrings. He had hesitated over the sale, going back and forth down the street and turning to change his mind again and again, but when the time came, he could not hand it over to be changed for cash. He had clung on to it so long, his minute haul, guarded it so jealously, nursed it so fiercely, that he could not let it go. So now, for all those months, those years of absence, he has these two small dabs of gold lying in his palm. He had thought that they might show her something of where he has been, of what he has seen, but of course they can't do that. He had thought they would be better than nothing, but now, holding out his handkerchief in the gloom of the room, he feels they are worse.

He closes the little gold balls into his fist and moves towards her. But she turns away again and busies herself with the tea, telling the boy to bring the chair over for his da. He can't imagine how he will take off his clothes and climb into the bed beside her when it gets dark, or put his arms around her, or find any way down the winding path back towards their intimacy when his failure hangs like this in the air between them.

He sits down heavily on the chair and presses the earrings into his palm so that when he opens his fist again, they have made two livid red marks in his skin. His wife brings him a mug of steaming tea and turns back to the stove.

When he looks up, he sees his son is watching him. For the first time they look properly at each other, weighing each other up. And then his son takes a few steps across the floor to him and in one sweep Huw pulls him up on to his knee, although he's too big for that now really, and his feet reach the floor. His hair smells musty, of sweat and wood smoke. They sit there together, both of them with their thin noses and sloping foreheads and uncertain gait, small and large versions of the same basic man. He leans back and closes his eyes and thinks about Ballarat, about the sunsets exploding across the horizon, in colours he had never seen. Unreal beauty. The way the world was there. The sea. The air. He doesn't have the words for it. And the men together, skin like leather under the sun. They sit there together in the dark room, and he puts one arm around the warm weight of his son and his other hand rubs over and over the little pair of gold balls, back and forth, as if they are a magic lamp from the story his wife used to tell their children, while his mug of tea cools slowly in the dank air.

Just Like Morse

A lone fox padded idly down the darkened lane, ears pricked and nose to the wind. He paused suddenly, sensing company, then skittered and bolted for cover as the silence was shattered by a startled cry.

'Aaaargh! Doh!'

'What the…?' Instantly alert, Sergeant Craddock sat bolt upright and peered keenly into the darkness. 'What is it, Hewitt? Did you see something?'

'Er… no. Sorry, Sarge. Spilt my coffee. Must have nodded off mid pour. Can we put the map light on?' He fumbled frantically in the door pocket for a cloth.

'Blimey, Hewitt. Are you sure you're in the right job? What do they teach you about stakeouts in training school?'

'Not a lot, Sarge, actually. All this heavy stuff is supposed to come later.'

'Maybe in the Met lad, but this is Badgers Bottom, remember. Short on serial killers and not much in the way of parking violations which, since there's only two of us, is just as well. But that's why, career wise, you get to climb the ladder a bit quicker.'

'I see, Sarge. So, the good thing is that, whatever comes up, I get to participate.'

'Yes, lad, and the bad thing is that, whatever comes up, you get to participate.'

'Sarge?'

'Never mind. Pass the coffee.'

A waft of steam misted the windscreen, and the sergeant wiped clumsily at it with one hand then peered out again, screwing up his eyes and tutting. 'Well, if he was out there, he won't be hanging about now. You've got a fine pair of lungs on you, Hewitt. I might not bother with the siren in future.' He swigged his coffee and tossed the dregs out the window. 'Come on. Let's call it a day. I'll drop you home.'

In the pub later, Sergeant Pete Craddock pondered this latest upset as the barman pulled him a pint of Old Toady. Before he picked it up, he scrutinised the beer to make sure it cleared. Not much got past him, but he was puzzled by this current business. If Margie Brewster was to be believed, there was a flasher in the spinney. Seems he'd surprised her twice now while she was out walking the dog, each time on a Thursday. 'Insulted her' was the way she'd put it. As crime in Badgers Bottom went, this was serious stuff. But no one else had come forward – yet.

Hewitt's notes were a bit sketchy to say the least, and he'd pulled him up on it.

'It's not much of a description, lad, is it – dirty raincoat. And did you ask her exactly what happened? I mean, 'opened raincoat and flashed' isn't very precise, is it?'

'She's eighty-nine, Sarge. She said a flasher had insulted her. She said he kept his… ahem, 'equipment' under there. I didn't like to press for too many details. Could be traumatic for someone that age, psychologically damaging even.'

Sergeant Craddock tossed the notes aside and let out a sigh. These modern kids had no idea how to conduct an interview. In his opinion, it would take a lot to traumatise Margie Brewster, or why had she been back for a second look?

Pete sipped his beer slowly, savouring it. She was a tough old bird, Margie. Anyone else would have changed their route. He looked around him. He thought he knew most of the people propping up the bar. More importantly, they knew him. It had probably been all round the village within the first hour that the entire Badgers Bottom police force was sitting across from the spinney in a borrowed car, trying to look inconspicuous. Could be they'd scared off their prey. He considered the spinney. It wasn't very big, little more than a cut through to the church really, but fairly well used. If you were looking to frighten someone, you wouldn't have to wait long. Anyone with local knowledge would know that. But it was hard to believe it was a local, and why Thursday each time?

The next day, he reviewed his notes and came up with a new plan. The car might well have been spotted or would be if they continued to park in the same place. Why not use Margie's house? It was right on the edge of the spinney, and the front room would have a good view along the path. No one need know they were there, and if Hewitt wanted to throw coffee over himself, he could go to the kitchen and do it.

Margie was thrilled. 'Oh, how exciting. It's just like Inspector Morse. Do you think he's dangerous then, this man?'

Sergeant Craddock rubbed his chin. 'Well Margie, no one's come to any harm yet, but who knows what this character might do next. We can only speculate.' Margie let out a little gasp and put her hands to her mouth. 'But...,' he patted her shoulder reassuringly, '...I don't want you to worry. I've got my crack team on the job.'

There was a clatter as Constable Hewitt's baton became entangled in Margie's umbrella stand. The sergeant glared at him. Hewitt's face wore an expression which said, 'I can't believe I did that.' The sergeant's expression said, 'Can't you? What, really?'

The constable grimaced and mouthed a silent 'sorry'.

Margie Brewster, hostess and chief witness, looked anxiously from one to the other.

'Don't mind young Hewitt,' said the sergeant. 'He's smarter than he looks. Got a degree, you know, in...' He paused, articulating each syllable with exaggerated care, '...psy...chol...o..gy.' He accorded it the same respectful tone he might have used for the word, 'em...broi...der...y' then sought confirmation. 'Isn't that right, Constable?'

'Yes sir. In fact, there's a theory about this sort of activity.'

The Sergeant interrupted. 'Yes, well, I have a theory of my own, Hewitt. It disgusts me. That's my theory. And I won't have it on my patch.'

'No, Sarge.'

'It is illegal then,' said Margie. 'I thought it should be. My Bertie was quite alarmed, weren't you Bertie?' On hearing its name, a woolly-headed creature of uncertain gene pool, but possibly owing something to a mix of poodle and dachshund, detached itself from the hearth rug and nuzzled her hand. She patted the head. 'Yes,' she said, 'nasty man.'

Sergeant Craddock and PC Hewitt set themselves up in Margie's bay window with the lights off. The moon was almost full, and as the light faded outside, the crack in the curtains gave a reasonable view of the path through the spinney. In the interests of health and safety, Margie was despatched to make some coffee while her crack team took it in turns to take watch. The first sign of a dodgy character and they'd be on him.

The minutes ticked by, and every so often someone would go in or out of the spinney. Mostly they were people they recognised: the vicar, an assortment of regular dog walkers, and the postman's wife with the bloke from the riding stables. Well, that was common knowledge. Sergeant Craddock could feel his left leg going to sleep and was beginning to wonder if this was such a good idea after all, when a cry went up from the kitchen.

'That's him, that's him. Sergeant, that's him.' Out in the lighted hall, Margie Brewster was wrestling her coat down from its hook and would have been out of the door if PC Hewitt hadn't jumped up in the dark and banged his head on the wall.

'Ow!'

Margie hesitated. 'Oh dear, are you alright? Oh, quick, quick. He's getting away.'

But Sergeant Craddock was out of the house ahead of her, bundling his dazed constable before him and urging her to stay put. 'Leave it to us now, Margie.' He signalled to Hewitt. 'He's not going to be in a hurry, I don't suppose. You run alongside the church and watch the other end of the path. I'm going in after him.'

Margie watched from the window for some time, and eventually her patience was rewarded. There was a scuffling at the edge of the spinney as the two policemen manhandled a man out of the trees and frogmarched him round the corner to where they had left the car. The man didn't look ready to go quietly and was blustering and gesticulating all the way.

Such a bad-tempered man, thought Margie, although she couldn't really hear what he was saying. That nice constable seemed to have pulled the man's raincoat down over his head and got the collar caught in his handcuffs. She could just about hear what the sergeant was saying though, something about, '…pig's ear of that, Hewitt'.

The man would probably be back fairly quickly, Margie thought, once he calmed down enough to explain himself. She'd seen the same sort of thing on Morse. Sometimes, like it or not, the police had no choice but to let these unsavoury characters go. Now that she'd had time to think about it, the photography club often used their Thursday meeting for outdoor work. The man would probably stand on his rights and say that it wasn't illegal to photograph badgers, or to keep your camera under your raincoat if it looked like rain, or to open it to take a picture. And that was all fair enough, she supposed. But Bertie wasn't to know that. That flashing had frightened him half to death, and there was no reason for the man to be quite so insulting. She could tell that nice young constable had been shocked. He'd gone quite pale when she'd told him how Bertie had launched himself at the man's equipment. But people got away with far too much these days. And the nerve of that photography club. The badgers were one thing but 'Ugliest Dog Competition'?

Bertie pressed himself against her legs and let out a single bark. She buried her fingers in his matted curls and scratched his head. 'Never you mind, Bertie. I expect that nasty man has learned a lesson anyway. People underestimate you when you're not good looking. They underestimate you when you're eighty-nine too. Still, first round to us, I think. 'Rabid old toilet brush' indeed.'

Showgirls

They gather around the Fountain; they kiss and hug and wait.

Eyes glued to their smartphones, the girls know that come six twenty-five Mr Black Audi will speed past the Fountain, his car horn blasting three times for each one of the young ladies. They will wave back. They will giggle. He is only eighteen but quite brawny. Unlike his dad - whom he helps at the pizzeria on weekends - furry chest, triple chin and beer belly. The girls picture him, his arms working the sticky dough, sweat pouring down his brow, wetting down his goatee, down to his tattooed neck - he is seeing someone, anyway. She is twenty-one, a full-time fashion student and a part-time beauty pageant. His dad does not approve. Neither do they.

The girls know that come six forty-five, Mr Ford Fiesta… 'Will he or won't he?' they bet. The girl with ashy blonde hair bets he will. The girl with the undercut bets he might. The girl with the belly button piercing bets he will not. It is Champions' League night, he will not. But they know, the girls know, it would be better for them if he did not. The last time he did, the matriarchs went on a crusade, knocking on their front doors, yelling at their mothers and their fathers that if they do not have the time to look after their children, and what are their children doing up so late on a school night, and that everybody can hear them, and the filth coming out of their potty mouths every time the Ford Fiesta stops by, engine roaring, and how that wannabe football player lures the children into his car, and how in God's name have they not noticed the Ford Fiesta disappearing into town at precisely six-fifty only to reappear again at twenty minutes to midnight.

It's five minutes past seven. They shrug their shoulders. Today the matriarchs have won the battle. But next

Wednesday, there will be another Wednesday.

The girls lace up their Converse shoes and smooth down their skirts. They wrap their hair in high ponytails and apply some lip gloss. The girls know their skirts are always too short, their hair always too bleached or too dark, their eye lashes too Rimmelled. The girls know their lips are too young for rouge, their bosoms too flat for crop tops, their legs too skinny for denim shorts and their ankles too bony for platform shoes. The girls know they are too young for vodka and orange, but too old for candies and Easter eggs. They are not old enough to drive, but young enough to be driven by their parents to and from house parties. The girls play some music on their phones and start practising their dance routine. Their feet and elbows move in choreographed sequences. Their movements are sharp, precise, and the girls do not miss a beat. Their backs twist, their hips turn, their buttocks squat, their foreheads sweat, to the sound of unintelligible tunes - about guys, and sex, and of course, violence. Because young girls only think about guys, and sex, and of course, violence, so they say. The girls take a break, dab at their faces with towels and take a sip of running water from the Fountain.

The girls know that come seven-fifteen, the last bus of the day will drop off Mr Woody. Mr Woody is old, ancient old, he is half-deaf and has recently undergone cataract surgery. The girls know Mr Woody will be dressed up in his Sunday best, will be carrying a heavy shopping bag and will be limping across the road with a walking stick as wooden as his right leg. The girls will wish Mr Bus Driver a good evening, flashing their cheekiest smiles knowing that this would be enough to turn his face crimson. Mr Bus Driver is in his early forties but with a chubby, almost baby face. On their way back from school, the girls know how to tease him. They know Mr Bus Driver has just come back from his honeymoon, they know his wife is a doctor, and they love how his baby face blushes violently when they point at the dark rings under his eyes, teasing him that someone did not get much sleep last night, wondering how and when he and wifey find the time to, you know, she always home so late and he up and ready at four-thirty in the morning. But they know, the girls know, not to step over the line. The girls respect Mr Bus Driver because when they need to let off some steam, he listens. To their teenage tantrums, to their broken hearts, to their stupid problems. Mr Bus Driver won't judge them if their skirts are too short, if their hair is blue, if Kanye is God, Beyonce is a goddess, if they do not care about politics, if they care about the planet and pandas and shoes and handbags. When the bus stops, the girl with ashy blonde hair helps Mr Woody step off the bus, the girl with the undercut grabs his bag brimming with groceries and the girl with the belly button piercing escorts him to the front door. Mr Woody smiles, God-blesses the girls, he will keep them in his prayers. The girls know what the matriarchs are going to tell their parents, that Mr Bus Driver is a married man now and that he should maybe be a little bit more careful when talking to school girls in front of other passengers, and how some passengers have already complained about the loud music and how school girls should be reading their text books instead of lousy text messages and how young girls today only dream to become showgirls.

'Dinner's ready!' hollers a voice across the road.

'Five more minutes, Mum!'

'I said, dinner's ready!' and so the girl with the undercut quickly packs up her belongings, then hugs and kisses and says goodbye to her girlfriends.

Her girlfriends protest. He is on his way, they plead. But the girl with the undercut shakes her head. Next Wednesday. There will be another Wednesday. Her girlfriends know what kind of mother hers is, and when she finds out about the maths test, there will be no more MTV, no more dancing and no more gathering around the Fountain. Next Wednesday. There won't be another Wednesday.

'Mazda o'clock!' the girl with the belly button piercing squeals as the girl with ashy blonde hair is already gasping for air. The girl with the belly button piercing knows how nervous her girlfriend is. She knows why her ashy blonde hair has been styled into bouncy curls, why the dangle earrings and the Mentos poking out of her denim jacket. She knows that nothing has happened between them, but it might as well happen this evening. Come seven-thirty, the girls know that the metallic blue Mazda will pave its entrance through the only road in the hamlet, and how the matriarchs will peek through their curtains, and when the Mazda pulls over the girl with the belly button piercing will kiss and good-luck and use-protection and text-me-later the girl with ashy blonde hair who will be whisked away to... Her girlfriend is seventeen and a half. She is almost a woman. He is a decent lad, of course she knows that, and how fast he has picked up the language. The girl with the belly button piercing has explained this to her parents - at least she has tried to - that not every olive-skinned man or woman who speaks Arabic was born a terrorist. That the Nigerian man selling bracelets and other sundries might be able to discuss quantum physics in two different languages, that not every Moldovan woman wearing high heels and a miniskirt walks the street, that not every Russian is a spy, that abortion is not a crime, and not every priest is a saint. She knows her parents understand that - at least they're trying to - but she also knows they, like everyone else in the hamlet, do wonder how he can afford a brand new metallic blue Mazda and diamond earrings, and flashy white Nike shoes when so many youngsters are on the dole, whereas he nearly died in a minefield five years ago. And when her heart is about to sink, she thinks of her older girlfriend who told her that she wants to become a human rights lawyer - and she will become a human rights lawyer, with the brains and the smile of Amal Clooney - and a rush of pride and euphoria goes straight into her head.

It's seven forty-five, and the lone girl with the belly button piercing decides it's time to go home. No luck tonight. Next Wednesday, there will be another Wednesday. She is about to put her big Bose on when she notices the white Fiat 500. Oh dear, she sighs. The car slows, its window lowering down. The pink rosary hanging on the rear-view mirror. 'Good evening, my child' and 'Good evening, Father' and 'Quite a balmy evening' and 'Indeed, Father' and 'How's school going?' and 'It's going alright, Father' and 'I didn't see you in church on Sunday' and 'I was busy studying, Father' and 'Even on a Sunday morning?' and 'Even on a Sunday morning' and 'How's your mum?' and 'She's fine, Father' and 'Are you being good to her?' and 'I think I am, Father' and 'You're heading home for supper?' and 'I am, Father' and 'What's that little thing on your navel, my child?' and 'It's a belly button piercing, Father' and 'How old are you?' and 'I'm almost sixteen, Father' and 'Did it hurt?' and 'Of course it did, Father. It's a hole in your belly' and 'What does your mum think of it?' and 'She hates it, she thinks I'm stupid and that I'm going to regret it' and 'Maybe you should've listened to your mother, my dear' he says.

'What if your mother is right?' he adds. 'What if you are going to regret it?'

The girl ponders.

'How about you, Father?'

'How about me, my child?'

'Did you listen to your mother when you were young?'

'Of course, I did. She would've smacked me if I hadn't.'

'And what did she think about it?'

'About what, my child?'

'Becoming a priest. That maybe you—'

But she stops.

She wishes Father goodnight.

She knows that he knows that girls her age only dream to become showgirls.

Punch Drunk

The Family

My mother's name is Judith, ironically. Never Jude and certainly not Judy. My father called himself the Professor, but that wasn't his name, of course, and as far as I know, he didn't work at a university. My mother was fifteen when she fell pregnant. My father wasn't. My mother was no better than she should have been, as they used to say. My father was a child abuser, although that's not how people thought about these things in the 1950s. My mother lost her virginity on Blackpool Promenade, inside a Punch and Judy tent. My father kept his left hand up Mrs Punch's skirt throughout it all, according to my mother. That's the way to do it! My mother tells me more than I want to know about these things when she's drunk.

Our family is what counsellors call dysfunctional. I am a bastard. My father never talks to me. Period. I've never had so much as a squawk out of him. He doesn't talk to Mum either. She drinks a lot these days, wine mostly: red, white, red, white, red... in memory of the tent perhaps. I'm guessing that my father was never much of a conversationalist. He worked with his hands after all. My mother lives in Bury these days. I live in London. My father lives somewhere other than Blackpool, or so I assume. He's been a ghost since 1957. My mother owns a dog, as you might imagine, but her dog doesn't like raw sausages. My mother doesn't like them either. They remind her of my father, apparently. On the plus side, my father has never thrown me across a room, nor beaten me with a stick. Or done anything else with me.

My mother is disappointed that the police have never taken an interest in the case. Until recently.

'I haven't got a bloody clue,' she said. 'He could be anywhere, love. Anywhere at all. But we've got to start somewhere, so this is where we are going to start.'

We? We?! I didn't really care if I never met the bloke. I just wanted a proper holiday like other kids in my class. I didn't want to go to Blackpool again. I certainly didn't want to march up and down the promenade each summer looking for Punch and Judy shows, nor when we found one, did I want to sit with the children shouting, 'He's behind you. Behind you!' until the show was over so that Mum could catch a glimpse of the puppeteer as he left the back of the tent.

'No, that's not him,' she would say. He was always shorter or taller, younger or older, less swarthy, monopedal. Whatever. He was never the Professor she remembered, although by the age of ten I was beginning to wonder if she could really remember him at all.

'What was he like, Mum?'

'Oh - he was, you know, handsome and attractive. Quite mature for his age. Well-educated, I'm sure. You know.'

I didn't.

Well-educated? He made a living by squatting in a tent with a swazzle in his mouth. Mature for his age? What age might that have been? I tried instead to imagine that we were playing 'Guess Who?', flipping tiles down to find my father by a process of elimination.

'Was his hair dark?'

'Well, darkish. But the light in the tent was poor.'

'Did he wear glasses?'

'I don't think so.'

'Did he have a beard?'

'Of course not. I don't like men with beards.'

'But he might have grown one since.'

'Oh, do shut up, Catherine. You're not helping. Let's try the amusement arcades. He might be having a break.'

And so it was that we spent our holidays, until my mother had a better idea.

The Professor

'I've had a better idea,' she said one day. It was 1975. I was seventeen years old.

She had been to the library and spoken at length to a recently divorced librarian who assured her that all men were indeed bastards and pointed her towards a magazine entitled, 'The Puppet Master', to which my mother now subscribed.

'It's full of useful stuff, Catherine. It tells you all about...' she decided to read from the cover, '...brings you up-to-date news about shows, festivals, workshops and exhibitions, and meetings around the country.'

She smiled at me, as if our troubles would soon be over, and finished her second glass of wine. It was almost lunchtime.

'So... we aren't going to Blackpool this summer!' she announced brightly.

I was delighted. Some of my friends at school were going to Spain. I was hoping we might bump into them.

'Can we go to Spain?' I asked.

'No, love. We're going to Harrogate. There's a big conference taking place. All the best puppeteers in the country will be there. I'm sure we'll find him this time. Then we'll be a proper family.'

Harrogate was cold that year. Cold and wet. We spent a lot of time inside the conference centre drinking coffee (or wine as the case may be) and attending talks and workshops: Story Development in Puppet Theatre; Bringing the Unseen to Life through Puppets; Acting by Proxy. And then she spotted it: Punching Above your Weight - Seeing the Past in the Present, a talk by Professor Fantasma.

'Fantasma?' I asked.

'Well, he could have been Italian. He was good looking. I don't know. It's probably just a stage name,' she said defensively.

The session was busy, and the room was full. A red-and-white striped tent had been erected on a small stage at the front of the lecture hall, and the lights were dimmed. It was going to be a theatrical presentation. We sat in the middle of the front row. I had rarely seen my mother this excited. A spotlight illuminated the tented proscenium. Mister Punch appeared in the bottom corner of the set, his head and body swinging wildly from side to side. The audience applauded. My mother inhaled noisily and stared at the gaudy puppet, leaning forward in her seat.

'Hello boys and girls!' squawked the puppeteer from inside the tent.

My mother turned to me with a messianic look in her eyes.

'It's him,' she whispered fiercely. 'It's him!'

The Black Dog

It wasn't him, of course. Professor Fantasma was a bearded Welshman who had never been to Blackpool. Besides, he was gay and always had been. He worked for Carmarthenshire County Council as a housing officer and lived with his mother. All of this we learned in an embarrassing fifteen minutes at the end of his talk.

My mother was devastated. She cancelled her subscription to 'The Puppet Master' and cut herself off from the world. She stayed in the house, drinking: red, white, red, white, red. She beat herself up (but not with a stick), and she cried a lot. It was difficult to know if they were crocodile tears, or for whom exactly she was crying. Herself, I assumed. So, I left her to it and went to university in London, 200 miles away. I told you I was a bastard.

When I returned at Christmas, I could see that things had taken a turn for the worse. The house was strewn with empty bottles and take-away cartons. She rarely left the house. The dog had been left to shit in the front garden, which fortunately was overgrown. Mum's wine was being delivered by the local ASDA supermarket. There were piles of cigarette butts in the ashtrays. My mother had been signed off work on an open-ended basis, suffering from depression. Her union claimed it was a disability, so her sick pay had been extended. I wasn't surprised that she was depressed. She spent most of her time in an old pair of pyjamas, lying on the sofa ordering goods on impulse from a shopping channel.

On Christmas day we ordered an Indian take-away and my mother opened a bottle of cheap champagne (in addition to all the usual stuff). It was a celebration, of sorts.

'Here's to family,' she said, raising her glass.

'Really, Mum, you've got to pull yourself together. Forget Dad. Move on. Stop drinking. Just... fucking do something with your life. I don't have to follow you around and look after you anymore, you know. I'm all grown up now, in case you haven't noticed.'

Two days later I left for London.

The Policeman

On the 18th February, 1982, Sergeant Markham called me. I remember the date because it was my mother's 40th birthday.

'Is that Mrs Catherine Williams? It's about your mother, Judith.'

'Drunk and disorderly?'

I was guessing. I hadn't seen my mother for five or six years, and I hadn't spoken to her since she failed to attend the wedding.

'Well, yes... but I'm afraid it's a bit more serious than that. She assaulted an officer with a cricket bat, and she's been detained under Section 3 of the Mental Health Act. She claims to have lost a baby as well, but there doesn't appear to be any reason to believe that. I'm sorry to trouble you with all this, but we haven't been able to contact her husband. He's a Professor of some sort, I believe. Is that right?'

'They separated a long time ago,' I said, not wishing to make my mother sound any more deranged than they already assumed her to be. 'I don't know where he is.'

'And the baby...?' he continued.

'No. No, there's no baby, Sergeant.'

The Baby

'I'm sorry, baby. It won't happen again,' said Judith.

Catherine was about to leave. She had returned to Bury for a couple of weeks in order to take care of her mother who had been released from the hospital on condition there would be someone at home to look after her.

'Look, Catherine, I know I haven't been the best mother in the world...'

'No.' Catherine stared at her.

'But I'm over it now. It's finished. I've stopped drinking and I can see that I've been ridiculous...'

'Only for the last twenty-five years,' interrupted Catherine.

'Yes. Well. I can see that what I've done... what I've done to you... and to myself... I can see that I've been foolish. It was wrong. I can see that now. I've messed everything up, haven't I? I know, but I just wanted a proper family, Cath. A real home. For you. And for me. You and me. I want to make it right, love. From now on, I mean. For the future.'

'The taxi's here, Mum. I've got to go.' Catherine pecked her mother on the cheek and turned away, avoiding her mother's embrace.

'Bye, love,' said Judith. 'Bye-bye b...' The taxi door closed, and the car pulled away.

Judith shut the front door gently and returned to the sitting room. The dog whimpered and she stroked it.

'There, there,' she said. 'At least we've got each other, eh? That's all we need, isn't it? Just you and me.'

She sat in silence for what seemed like a long time. The sun set and the room darkened. She opened the laptop which was sitting on the coffee table in front of her. It defaulted to Google which told her that it was the 21st of March. World Puppetry Day. The cursor was blinking in the search box. She pulled the laptop closer and began to type: 'ASDA home delivery'.

The Friend

He didn't usually linger once he'd bought his morning paper - why spend money eating out when there was a perfectly good cup of tea and a biscuit waiting at home? He might, if the weather was good, sit on a bench on the seafront but not to read as it was impossible, even in a slight breeze, to keep the pages still but just to relax and take in the view. Thus, more often than not, he went straight back to the chalet he had rented for two months every year for the past five years since his wife had died – August, when he enjoyed watching the holiday makers arrive and September, when he enjoyed seeing them go.

This year, however, was different. His doctor had advised him not to go away at all, but he had just shrugged and flapped a hand in the air.

'If it's my last, it's my last,' he had said. 'In fact, I will make it three months and leave in July.'

The paper bought, he was on his way back when a strong wind accompanied by a heavy shower of rain sprung up from nowhere and literally blew him into the doorway of the EatSumMor Café, and as he leant against the door to gain more shelter, Selina on the other side opened it so that he fell against her, his walking stick clattering onto the floor.

It was when she put out her hand to steady him and pick up the fallen stick that he noticed the scar on her wrist and later, when she came with his cup of tea, the scar on the other wrist, plus the blue, purple and yellow colouring around one eye and cheek.

She, in turn, when he took off his gloves (he always wore gloves when fetching the paper, whatever the weather) and laid them neatly on the table to where she had guided him, noticed the tattooed numbers on his wrist.

'There you are, love,' she said. 'One tea and a Chelsea bun.' She looked out of the window. 'What a downpour! Luckily, it's passing. Look there's a rainbow!'

After that he had his elevenses - at 10 o'clock - every day at the same table reserved for him by the window, overlooking the pier. As the weeks of his holiday slipped by, Selina's bruises varied in size and colour and sometimes were not there at all, although the scars on the wrists were permanent.

They passed the time discussing the weather, the state of the country, the state of the town and how quiet it would be in the winter months. It took a while before she talked about herself - she never elaborated on the cause of the bruises and he didn't ask. Feeling more at ease with him, she told him that she had no children and a husband who was out of work. It was now the holidays, but she had been going to evening classes to study for a degree in English Literature.

'I'm a mature student,' she told him, although at forty-five was not the oldest in the class. 'They are a friendly crowd and the lecturer, Mr Martin, is great. He makes the classes really interesting.' He noticed a slight change in her voice and that her eyes lit up when she said this.

'The course has changed my life. I've always loved books and reading. I've written some short stories. Would you like to see them? I would value your opinion, good or bad. I write here at the cafe when it's quiet.' She paused. 'It's better than writing at home. Fewer distractions. Anyway, my husband only reads The Racing News. He thinks books are a waste of time.'

In turn he told her he was nearly 90 ('You don't look it,' she said) and Polish by birth. In 1945, when he was 15, he had escaped from a train transferring people from one camp to another. This was the last time he had seen his mother, sister and younger brother; his father had already disappeared. Tears came to Selina's eyes at this.

It was the closing months of the war, and eventually he was picked up by the Allies and sent to England where he was placed with a loving family. 'Very loving,' he said with a twinkle in his eye. 'I later married the daughter!'

When he was 17, he told her, he had joined the British Army and, when eligible, applied for and was accepted by the SAS. He also had no children, and, after leaving the Army, he and his wife backpacked 'to wherever their hiking boots took them'.

In Poland he found no trace of his family, so, wanderlust sated, they settled in Hereford where he made bespoke furniture, mostly hand carved.

'I learnt the carpentry skill whilst in the Army. I'm good with these,' he said, spreading out his hands on the table - it was a warm day and he had for once, abandoned the gloves.

Selina remarked on the walking stick with its intricate carved patterns and handle, shaped like the head of a swan. She had admired it from the first day they met.

'Yes,' he said. 'I made this. I call it my friend.'

September came, and with it the number of visitors dwindled, although the cafe was still popular with the locals. Selina returned to classes, and he looked forward to discussing the books which had been set for that term. Then, two weeks before he was due to return home, she was not at work. She had been absent before for a day, but when she was still not there the following day, he became concerned. And then there was a new waitress too, he noticed.

'No Selina?' he enquired of Karen, the owner of the café.

Karen hesitated, then the words came tumbling out. 'She's in hospital. Her husband accused her of having an affair, said she'd been meeting someone in secret. Well, he's always doing that, he's got such a nasty, jealous mind. It's a wonder he let her work here, knowing she would meet all sorts of people and her being so friendly.'

She paused and looked around her, as if she were afraid of being overheard. 'But he's really done it this time. Pushed her down the stairs - broken ribs, wrist and leg. The neighbours called the police and he spent the night in the cells, but he was released this morning. I don't know why she doesn't leave him. She won't be back at work for a while, I'm afraid.'

He felt himself go rigid, and his breath came sharply and quickly. His chest tightened as long buried emotions welled up inside him. He saw his mother pinned against the side of the wagon by a German guard, blood from her nose and mouth where she had been struck, the terrified look on her face as a knife was held to her throat. He had been big and tall for his 15 years, but he still did not know where the strength had come from to grab the knife, now in his hand.

He saw again the look of horror on the guard's face as the blade plunged into him. Nothing was said by the other occupants. Silently the wagon door opened, the body pushed out. And then he felt himself falling – was he also pushed? – and his mother's voice, 'Run Maurice, run.' Maurice had run.

'Are you all right? said Karen. 'You look a little pale. Here's your stick. You've knocked it off the table.'

That afternoon he visited Selina in hospital. He took her some books and some flowers. It had been a long time since he had bought flowers for anyone and he had spent a happy time choosing a selection, much to the amusement of the florist assistant who was trying to guess the recipient.

A nurse took the flowers to put in a vase. He put the books on top of a pile already on her locker and sat down. There were already flowers there, he noticed. 'Well,' was all he said.

Selina tried to smile. She was obviously in pain, but her eyes beneath the puffiness were bright. She turned her head towards the books and spoke slowly through split lips.

'You've just missed Tom, Mr Martin, my lecturer. Thank you for these, but I might be a while finishing them. I can't turn the pages at the moment!'

'No need to hurry,' he told her. 'I might come back for a few days in the New Year.'

Although he knew he probably wouldn't.

'I suppose you know what happened?'

Maurice nodded and, after a moment's pause, said, 'Why don't you leave him? It isn't a case of "til death do us part," is it?'

Selina shrugged. 'He always says he's sorry,' she said.

They talked for a while and when he could see that she was tiring, said his goodbyes and promised to keep in touch. As he turned to go, he caught sight of the chart at the end of her bed. He picked it up and memorised her address. He didn't go straight home, but when he did get back to the chalet later that evening there was a letter waiting from the hospital in Hereford and that made up his mind. He twisted the swan-shaped handle of his stick and pulled. The concealed blade flashed in the light.

It was never discovered who had killed Selina's husband. Not Selina, of course, for she was in hospital.

'Good riddance,' the neighbours said. 'He was always getting into drunken fights. Someone must have followed him from the pub and knifed him on the doorstep.'

The police kept an open file. There were no clues and no witnesses, but it was noted that whoever had done it was a professional. The blade had struck once, and once was all that was required.

The week before Christmas, Selina stood at the bay window of her flat overlooking the esplanade, front door keys with the estate agent's tag still attached clutched in her hand. She squeezed her eyes shut and opened them again. The lights were still there twinkling on the pier, the bright moonlight dancing on the waves breaking on the shore.

She had not seen Maurice again after the hospital visit. He had sent her more flowers (he had so enjoyed choosing again) with a note saying he had to return early to Hereford but would see her next year. He had heard of her husband's death and hoped that life would now be easier for her.

On the back of the note he had written a quote from Shakespeare's Julius Caesar, 'Cowards die many times before their deaths. The valiant only taste of death but once.'

When, in early October, she had opened the letter from the solicitors in Hereford, the quote came back to her. Maurice had left his money to various charities, but to her he had bequeathed his house and contents, 'to do with as you wish, as

I know that you will always want to live by the sea.'

It was not a large house - she had sold it easily with some of the contents - but the books and the furniture, mostly made by Maurice, she had kept.

Selina turned as the lounge door opened. Tom Martin came into the room and joined her at the window. He set down the tray he was carrying, put his arms around her and kissed her.

'Tomorrow at 10 o'clock we'll have tea and a Chelsea bun, but tonight, champagne,' he said, handing her a glass.

She walked over to the bookcase and picked up a photograph of the walking stick, which had been enclosed with the solicitor's letter.

'It's a pity you never saw this,' she said. 'It was beautifully carved. But his request was to have it cremated with him. He called it his friend.'

They clinked glasses and raised them.

'To you, Maurice. And your friend.'

Big Truth

I sat behind the counter reading Space Gorillas vs. Black Hole Alligators.

The book was a let-down. It was just a series of unconnected, increasingly outlandish space battles.

I put the book down and looked at the door. We hadn't had a customer in all day, and barely any this week. The laundromat I worked at was on a back street in an old building with paint peeling off the front. The washing machines lining the walls were old and industrial-looking.

I glanced at the clock and thought about sneaking a rip off the bong I had stashed under the counter.

The bell over the door dinged, and a woman with wild hair poked her head in. 'Hey, bro. The sign outside says, 'Free coffee'?'

Her name was Leilani. Everyone around here knew Leilani.

'Uhh,' I said, 'it means free coffee for customers.'

The coffee scheme had been the owner, Mr Kittler's, idea, to bring in more customers.

'Oh…' Leilani said. Then her face brightened. 'Tell you what, bro! You let me have a cup of coffee and I'll tell you the truth.' She said the last words like they had great significance.

I chuckled. 'What truth?'

'The big truth, bro.' She looked serious.

We looked at each other.

Six months earlier, Leilani had come into the laundromat and asked to use the bathroom. Mr Kittler had glanced at the other customers in the place and begrudgingly let her use the facilities. On her way out, Leilani had dipped a hand into a woman's laundry basket and grabbed a handful of clothing, then dashed out the door.

The woman had ultimately decided not to call the police.

But Kittler had said that if Leilani ever came back, I was to call them right away.

'Alright,' I said, starting to come around the counter. 'You can have a cup of coffee, but then...'

'Awesome!' Leilani came all the way in. She was holding a leash with a brown and white bulldog on the end. The dog's claws clacked on the lino as it plodded in and looked around.

Leilani herself wore a knitted sweater with holes in the sleeves and sweatpants with a pocket torn off.

I walked over and poured Leilani a cup of coffee. When I turned back, she was sitting on one of the plastic chairs in the middle of the room. Her dog was sniffing around under the chairs.

I went and gave Leilani the paper cup. She took it and blew on its surface with chapped lips.

I hesitated. Now would be the time to tell Leilani that, after she drank her coffee, she had to go.

'I used to have a bulldog,' I said instead, squatting and reaching a handout to the dog.

The bulldog sniffed my hand, gave it a prompt lick, then returned to its investigation of the floor under the seats.

'Yeh?' Leilani said, craning to look through her legs at the dog, 'Burt here is a big sleeper. Might say his snore is worse than his bite!' She whooped a laugh.

As though in response, the dog walked a small circle, then lay down with its head on its paws.

'What happened to your pup then?' Leilani asked.

'My ex took him when she moved out.'

'Why did she move out?'

I shrugged. 'Buggered if I know.' I got up, went back behind the counter and picked my book back up.

Leilani finished her coffee and put the cup down on the seat next to her.

I ran my eyes over words on the page, trying to make it clear that it was time to go.

'Doesn't matter about your ex anyway, bro,' Leilani said then. 'Because this whole thing is a simulation anyway.'

I looked up. 'What thing?'

'This world.' Leilani indicated the room around her, then nodded to me. 'And everyone in it. That's that big truth I mentioned before.' Leilani's face remained even. 'And you know what else, bro? I'm one of the ones who made the simulation. I'm a planner.'

I looked back down at my book.

'But I'm not the only one.' She gestured towards the window. 'There are loads and loads of planners out there. They live among you simulated fellas and no one notices a thing.'

I ran my eyes over words on the page, ignoring her.

'We simulated you guys to make mistakes. Yous mess up so others don't have to.'

I didn't look up.

'Thing is…' Leilani said. 'Something went wrong with your simulation. Really wrong.'

There was a long moment of silence. Leilani looked about the room nonchalantly.

Eventually, I sighed and put my book down.

'Alright,' I said. 'What went wrong?'

Leilani's face split into a smile. I saw she had a gold front tooth.

'Tell you what,' she said. 'You sort us out a feed and I'll tell you all about it.'

Leilani slurped at the cup of instant noodles I'd gotten from the back cupboard.

I watched her from the counter and mused on how stupid this was of me.

'Yous were supposed to terminate a hundred years ago,' Leilani said without looking up from her meal.

'Terminate?'

'Yeah, the simulation was supposed to shut down. But it got buggered up.'

The bell dinged, and a young woman came in with a bag of laundry.

I straightened and gave her a welcoming nod.

The woman smiled back, then turned to a machine. The sleeping dog lifted its head and glanced in her direction.

'I know what you're thinking,' Leilani murmured from her chair as she finished off the last of the noodle soup, 'Yous were created to make mistakes.' So, it makes sense that you failed to terminate properly.'

The customer at the washing machine glanced between Leilani and me.

'But nah…' Leilani shook her head gravely. 'It wasn't meant to be like that. Yous were supposed to show us how civilizations fail and stuff. Not mess up the natural order.'

The customer was furrowing her brow at Leilani.

I felt a pang. What if she told Mr. Kittler?

Leilani, oblivious, continued.

'When yous had that "great war" a hundred years ago? That was your termination point. But something went wrong and most of yous came out of it alright. Yous have been living as a glitch ever since, bro. Why d'you think you all feel like life lacks purpose now?'

The customer was watching Leilani openly now.

'That was the first time a simulated race had avoided termination,' Leilani continued. 'A lot of the other planners are scared of yous.'

She looked up then and smiled, showing her gold tooth.

'Not me though, bro! I think yous are alright.' She waved a hand. 'Those other planners are just wussies.'

The woman by the washing machine cleared her throat.

Leilani turned, then cried out and pointed a finger at the customer. 'She'll tell you, bro!' She was bouncing in her seat. 'Cos she's a planner just like me!'

The woman looked between Leilani and me slowly, then bent and began taking her clothes back out of the machine.

The bell dinged again as she left.

I bowed my head.

'See, bro?' Leilani said. 'Bunch of wussies.'

I was checking that the machines were empty in preparation for closing.

I glanced at Leilani, who was now sitting cross-legged on the floor and fondling the bulldog's ear. Now would be the time to tell her that she couldn't come back – that the owner didn't want her here.

'If the planners are afraid of us,' I said instead, 'then why don't they just pull the plug?' I straightened. 'If you guys turned us on, surely you can turn us off again.'

Leilani shook her head. 'Not that easy, bro. Like I said, all the other worlds we've simulated have shut themselves down like they were programmed to. We're not used to this.'

The dog let out a contented groan in response to Leilani's rubbing.

'But we're not dummies.' Leilani tapped her temple. 'We always put a switch somewhere in the simulation just in case the thing has to be shut down manually.'

I listened.

'Thing is, by the time we realised you guys hadn't shut down, you'd built all these roads and big buildings, and the switch was buried. And 'cos everything looked different, we couldn't find where we'd put it.'

'So that's why you've got so many planners down here?' I asked. 'They're looking for the switch?'

Leilani nodded. 'You got it, bro.'

I went to empty the coffee pot.

'They're getting pretty desperate to find the switch,' Leilani continued. 'Yous have developed a whole lot in the last hundred years. What with nuclear bombs and space travel and all that.'

I watched the black coffee trickle down the plughole.

'Yous are getting smarter. The planners are worried that if you ever realise the truth, you'll find a way to come after us.'

I set the empty coffee pot down.

'Some even say that creating yous to make mistakes was actually the biggest mistake we ever made. How's that for ironic, bro?'

Leilani's whoop of a laugh rang through the laundromat again.

I stepped out into the night and Leilani followed, pulling the dog after her. She produced a battered pack of cigarettes, removed one and lit it.

There was no one else on the street.

'So, what happens in the end?' I asked as I locked the doors.

Leilani was blowing smoke rings that looked like mangled calamari. Her dog sat down next to her with a plop.

'Eh?' she asked.

'What happens?' I said, turning to her. 'Do the planners find the switch? Or do the simulated humans find out the truth and do something about it?'

Leilani looked at me. Her eyes blinked rapidly.

'Did I tell you about the planners, bro?'

I nodded uncertainly. 'I mean, yeah...'

Leilani chewed her lip. Her cigarette dangled, forgotten, from her fingers.

'They're... they're all wussies, bro. Did I tell you that bit?'

She was breathing fast now.

'What about the mistakes... the... you gotta make the mistakes, and then...' Leilani's eyes were darting about.

Next to her, the dog stood up and craned its neck to lick the tips of Leilani's fingers. As he turned his head to lick from all angles, Leilani focused in on the dog's flat, creased face and her breathing began to slow.

Thinking it would be best if I left, I turned and started away.

I made it about five steps down the street before Leilani's voice rang out.

'Hey, bro!' she called.

I turned back.

'Did I ever tell you about how humans are gods who got depressed and came to earth to forget?'

I looked at the scruffy woman standing on the footpath for a long moment.

Then I shook my head. 'I don't think you did.'

'Maybe I could come by tomorrow and tell you about it?'

I smiled. 'Yeah, alright.'

Leilani cracked a big grin. Her gold tooth glimmered in the light of a streetlamp.

We walked off in different directions, Leilani chatting away to the dog at her side.

Chives are Onions Too

Peeling onions never brought a tear to Angela's eye. Chopping and sautéing those pearlescent globes, releasing their abrasive aroma and watching crisp white cubes turn to translucent, gold tinged petals was, for her, the start of an exotic journey. When the ladies of the Women's Institute rhapsodised about Rhine cruises and weekends in Seville, Angela's thoughts drifted to recipes. She devoured cookery books like novels. Every ingredient, a character. Each instruction, the plot. The gratifying denouement, the tinny sound of forks scraping plates clean. Until Ella.

Four of her five children married well into neighbouring farming folk. Not Rupert. Angela's autumn baby sidestepped agricultural college to go travelling. Chewing her nails between Facebook postings, Angela discovered her son sheep shearing in New Zealand, fish farming in Indonesia and 'having a blast' at an organic co-operative in California. Here he met Ella. 'I hope you'll like her as much as I do Mum,' he had emailed, detailing dates and times of their forthcoming visit.

Blowing a dusting of flour from the laptop keyboard, she surveyed the Facebook photo of her son, bearded and bronzed, his arms clamped around Ella's coat hanger shoulders. The white-haired girl, teeth bared in a blaze of haute couture dentistry above which cheek bones jutted like alpine ledges, was thin as linguini. 'We'll be fattening you up, young lady,' thought Angela.

Like tribes who regard plump women as a symbol of wealth, skinny was an insult to Angela. Her family, including Bill and Ben the honey-coloured Labradors, and Dumpling the cat, were all, thanks to her culinary prowess, comfortably clad. Nobody left Angela's table without a second helping. In anticipation of Rupert and Ella, she cooked as if for a siege.

Strapping on her gravy stained apron, Angela gathered knives, sieves and scales on the long pine table where Dumpling licked his nether regions. Pies and pasties, cakes and buns were loaded into the Aga. Like her kitchen, with its scratched work surfaces and cracked 1970's wall tiles featuring grey windmills, she'd inherited the grease laden Aga when she married Phil all those years ago.

Her late mother-in-law's sunken soufflé of an armchair, its faded chintz pattern obscured by dog hair and mud, sat beside the bowed leaded window, through which damp drafts dissipated the aroma of home baking and sent pet hair balls bowling across the flagstones, catching up mouse droppings in their wake. Rimmed with green mould and draped with ivy, the window obscured views across the cobbled farmyard where puddles formed from torrential rain. So absorbed was Angela in piping Welcome Home on the iced fruit cake, she did not hear the taxi arrive. Rupert, stooping as he entered the back door, surprised her with a 'Hi Ma'.

Angela felt his beard scratch her face as he kissed her. But where was her cuddly lad? Beneath his shirt, she felt firm muscle. His skin glowed. He smelt of limes. 'And this,' she heard her alien son say with a faint Californian twang, 'is Ella.' Angela approached the waif-like woman with arms outstretched. Careful not to hug too hard lest she snap a rib, she stepped back from the embrace to see icing-sugar fingerprints on Ella's fringed black bomber jacket.

'I'm like, so pleased to meet you, Angela,' Ella said with sing-songy Hollywood familiarity. At that moment, soaking wet dogs crashed in, unbalancing Ella's sapling figure. Spattering mud up the walls like a cut-throat crime scene, they swept up aluminium bowls in slobbering chops, scattering dog food pellets to the four corners. 'Don't mind the boys,' said Angela, picking up her icing bag, 'they've done that since they were puppies, haven't they Rup?' Ella bent to wipe brown smears from her white jeans.

118

'Rupert, show Ella her room.' Angela registered Ella's quizzical raised pale eyebrow, 'And we'll pop those jeans in the washing machine whilst I make us all a nice cup of tea.'

'I'm afraid I don't drink English tea,' said Ella. 'There are studies showing it could be carcinogenic and anyway, I'm lactose intolerant. I always travel with organic fruit infusions.'

'You don't drink milk, dear?' inquired Angela, incredulous.

'Yeah, no dairy. Like it's kinda weird when I know you're dairy farmers. And, I guess we should have said, but I also have an issue with wheat. So, bread's out, pasta, stuff like that. I've brought my own rice cakes. And do you have a blender? I gotta whiz up my superfood cocktail. Don't worry, I always travel with Reishi powder. Never go anywhere without it.'

Angela backed away as if Ella were the undead. 'That must be so difficult for you, dear,' she offered.

'Yeah, it's the reason I went vegan. I was vegetarian because I'm like so not open to animal cruelty. But vegan is where I'm at now.' Angela cast her eyes towards the rain-lashed barn where bull calves surplus to requirements awaited the abattoir. She listened while Ella droned through a long list of foodstuff to which she was 'intolerant' including, the king of vegetables, onions. 'Man, they bring on my IBS.'

Angela thought of the onion-based meals piled up in her chest freezer. 'I could make you a nice quiche,' she offered.

Ella turned down thin lips and said, 'Like I said, pastry, eggs, cheese. No can do.'

'What do you live on, dear? Dust?' Rupert shot her a wounding, warning look. Ella, occupying an irony free zone, ploughed on, 'Don't you worry about us, Ang. We'll just do our own food thing.'

'We?' Angela queried, looking at the welcome home cake now rendered inedible to Ella as sultanas made her skin 'come up in, like, weals'.

'Ella inspired me to go vegan too, Mum. Sorry if we've put you to any trouble.'

In the days that followed, Angela's family and friends,

dropping in for homemade biscuits and lemon drizzle cake, found Ella and Rupert wiping down surfaces with disinfectant before preparing dishes of what looked like cement. Ella, her little nose wrinkling with undisguised disgust, shoed Dumpling off the table and banned the dogs from the kitchen. 'Ella needs a hygienic environment, Mum,' Rupert said gently. 'Otherwise, it brings on her hives.'

A tour of the farm ended with Ella running to her room in tears. 'You can't kill those poor little calves,' she wailed. 'Like, it's so cruel.' Angela tried to explain the ways of a working farm, but Ella's world view was pure West Coast. Fox hunting? Trembling lips. Badger culls? Fists in eyes howling. A trip to a local market? Silent tears at the sight of ducks and rabbits for sale in cages. It was a good job Angela always kept a packet of tissues in her bag.

On Sunday, as the family chomped through Baron of Beef and all the trimmings, Ella and Rupert produced chopsticks and pecked at a mound of leaves a hibernating hedgehog would have appreciated. During a discussion of cowboy films, Ella announced she could not 'sit at a table where "native Americans" were called Red Indians' and fled, adding the smell of dead meat made her 'sick to the stomach'.

With not an ounce of fat on her, Angela was not surprised Ella complained of being cold. Indoors she wore a duvet round her shoulders like a cloak and hunched over the fire in the sitting room piling on logs. 'How do you exist in this climate without central heating or proper insulation?' she whined. You could do with both, my girl, thought Angela, wondering why her baby chose this photographic negative of a woman.

Leafing through vegan recipes, Angela planned their farewell supper. A nut roast she decided. Intolerant to almost everything else on this green earth, Ella considered nuts a 'total superfood.' And since Ella had been driving Angela nuts ever since she arrived, what could be more appropriate? Nuts roasted, pearl barley simmered, mushrooms sizzled, parsnips mashed, and chives chopped into fine emerald specks. It smelled like silage and looked like cow cake, thought Angela posting the loaf tin into the Aga.

Whilst Rupert's brothers, sisters, nieces and nephews pushed nut roast round their plates, Ella and Rupert tucked in with enthusiasm. Angela, finally, felt a flush of pride.

Waking that night to the sound of doors banging and a lavatory flushing, she pushed feet into slippers and opened her bedroom door. Ella, even more wraithlike than usual, was coming back from the bathroom. 'Are you ill, dear?' Angela inquired.

'You put onions in that nut roast, didn't you? I know you don't like me, but you didn't have to try to poison me.' Mentally, Angela checked through the ingredients. No onions. But then she remembered, with some satisfaction, chives are onions too.

There is Life at This Level

Alex lives on the fifteenth floor. She doesn't take the lift, not even with the old-lady shopping trolley full of essentials - and vodka - she lugs up the stairs. She never thought a pandemic would get her fit, but her arms have curves now, and she likes those curves, not like the curves of her belly.

Stephen liked all her curves, even the curves of her belly, but that was a different time when he could lay his hands on her and she on him. That was a different time, when the lift was just a way to transport from one floor to another, fifteen flats higher, a shortcut that sometimes smelled of piss. Now it is not a lift, it is a petri dish of disease, of buttons pressed by dirty hands where the virus can linger for 72 hours, where someone else could step into the enclosed space and cough, danger, red, do not use the lift. She never uses the lift.

It is the same lift. It is the times that have changed. Circumstances. She likes that word, it sounds Jane Austen, when people danced with strangers, touched, strolled together, kissed.

The stairs are not part of the allocated hour's exercise outside. Alex can leisurely walk down being careful not to touch the handrail and crawl exhaustedly, slowly, up the stairs, because it is at the building's exit that you log out. There was a flaw in this plan, and there were friends and family and lovers in this block who went freely from households, laughing in groups, from one residence to another, shutting and opening doors, ushering in people, and the virus people carry with them. She doesn't hear them now. In the beginning of the new times Alex knew a lot of her neighbours and would leave food and medicine for them as required. This was charity not friendship though, none of the sick people would ever be well enough to do the same for her. But now it comes through the system and if she were sick the system would do this for her. It is not food and medicine she's hungry for though. She takes a deep breath in before logging out at the exit door to start the minutes ticking. Sixty minutes, contactless at the wall, as soon as it beeps, she begins to run, her body flooding with adrenaline, the fight she has every day, firing up her sympathetic nervous system.

She goes left, she always goes left, it is the same route each time, but it is the times that have changed. Past Abu Bakar, which is an essential shop and still open daily though the essentials in the shop vary considerably in usefulness; now she can reach there in 2 minutes flat which means she can get to the corner of the park in 10.

At the corner of the park is a pussy willow, strangled by ivy. The buds are all coming out, fluffy like a squirrel's tail. She spies a grey in the distance, reaching up on a beech tree with arms and legs splayed like Jesus on the cross. The willow is as busy as Friday night pubs were; there's a flock of tits - great, blue and long tailed - shouting at each other and nibbling amongst the ivy. The blackbirds have a nest like a flat above the pub, but they're not in it, they are calling each other at a distance. Alex breathes. She's got out, she feels present.

Alex only feels present at this hour when she gets to be outside. It starts here at the corner of the park with the willow, where she stretches, bends down on one thigh with the other leg outstretched, really low, so she can smell the grass. There is life at this level - a harlequin ladybird flaunts its bully body in all her garish freedom on a stem of grass. Alex puts her hand in her pocket and lifts up, brings out the packet of seeds that she scatters on the makeshift feeder ledge she bolted onto the tree last year. The birds recognise her now, she's sure of it, they know when she's there bent down to the ground, and they start chattering with increased excitement. Al-ex, Al-ex she imagines she hears. Every day she hears them say her name, up close like this, unfettered by a screen.

Alex feeds the birds stealthily and then runs on. They are not her only love. If she didn't have so little time she could step back and watch them come, the blue tits dangling upside down, the sparrows swarming in numbers like an army, sometimes with them a siskin, as subtle as herself when she bends the knee. She doesn't wait to watch but runs from them now as if she doesn't care, though every two weeks she carries seed up the stairs with her shopping, so she can have this single moment with them. Alex stuck a feeder to her window last month, but they never came.

It is up the hill she goes, and in the beginning, she couldn't make it in the allocated time. It was only two months ago her timer buzzed at her wrist, and she ran back screaming with frustration that she wouldn't see him, and sobbing so loudly past the feeder tree, her birds swarmed into the air and away from her as if they did not know her after all. Like souls leaving their bodies, she thought, at a site of a massacre. Or a pandemic. How old-fashioned, she thinks, a pandemic. As if we are just flesh and blood and mortal after all. As if we too will wither come age and disease. As if we are born and then die, sometimes too soon, often too soon.

Alex runs past the rotten beech that she used to sit under. Twenty-two minutes, good, she has time to unfasten her water bottle and drench her dry throat, and time to note the lichen growing upon the elderly beech; there are holes up and down this old boy, like pock marks from a different disease in a different time. And hoof fungus, as if inside there is a white stallion about to leap forth. Alex says hi to the beech, and there's a fast tap tap tap back that takes her by surprise.

She looks up and there's a woodpecker drilling at her beech. Brazen. She doesn't know much about birds, she just knows she can't live without them. After this run she will look up greater spotted and lesser spotted and still not know, but for now she just looks up at the real planeless sky and squints against the spring sun, and there is the white, black and red of whatever woodpecker he is, telling a potential partner he is up for it, or telling her to go away. She goes away. Her eyes are watering and she isn't sad.

Not yet.

At 26 minutes, she is by the gorse bushes that lead to Stephen. She breathes the scent in, lurid coconut, and with her eyes shut she remembers that Thai restaurant with him when he told her that joke, and she snorted very spicy soup out through her nose. And she breathes in again and tells the gorse that she still has her sense of smell. The gorse does not reply, but it carries on reeking of glorious exotic coconut.

Smell is another thing that goes, with the virus.

Perhaps Alex is still crying a bit, her face is definitely red and hot as if she has a fever.

It's now she can start to talk to Stephen.

She walks towards the gravestone. It is simple and small, and before he died, he joked with her that he wanted one like that because he was. She had cried then too, but she had been touching him because that was allowed then, she was holding his hands and they were both crying because cancer, they said, really sucks.

'Trust you,' she says to him now, 'to die of cancer when everyone else is about to die of coronavirus.'

There are still other diseases, he would have said.

Alex sits cross-legged on his grave and checks the time. Twenty-eight minutes. She has 5 whole minutes with him, it is quicker on the way back. A whole 30 seconds more than yesterday. She leans against his headstone as if it were his arms, and they were in bed, as they so often used to be.

'It never felt we had enough time then either,' she says. The stone is hard and inflexible, not like him, not like the warmth and softness of him. Even when he grew skeletal, she liked to lean on him, or him on her.

The pandemic reached Europe during his last days. They shared memes about it, next to each other, on their phones. They laughed together a lot in his last days, as serious about processing loss as any tears were. Alex knew that privately some people thought her frivolous for it. Stephen didn't though, and as he disappeared, pound of flesh by pound of flesh, he was all that mattered to her.

Alex realises they are not alone. There's a fox, skinny as Stephen in his last weeks, russet brown coat, white with mange. The fox is strolling across the graveyard like he owns it; he stops to sniff at a dried bouquet on another of this year's dead. Alex sits there quietly, still, an interloper. When he sees her, he doesn't run. She does though - it's 33 minutes and the buzzer goes.

Alex kisses the cold grey headstone and wishes it smelled like Stephen's unwashed hair.

Here she goes, back again, her face less red, though the ache is going to come to the thighs. Past the gorse bush, where she breathes it in again and says goodbye, and through the ginnel into the park. From afar she can see another runner all in black and slower than her, puffing up the hill. Alex waves and the runner waves. The wave means both a cheery hello and a hostile do not come near me. Alex smiles to emphasise the former - as probably the runner does - but neither will see the warmth of the other. It is important to maintain our humanity in these moments, Alex thinks. And out of the blue she imagines Stephen next to her hearing her, and he punches her on the arm to mock her earnestness and then Alex is laughing and the other anonymous runner may or may not hear the lonely chuckling of a woman who for this second doesn't feel alone.

Alex is past the beech tree and can't hear the woodpecker this time and then she's careering down the hill towards the feeder tree, and the little birds are all still there flocking in their gangs with such disregard. Oh, and suddenly, there's a scuffle in the tree right near the feeder as she arrives, and a kestrel lurching, claws out, swoops at her head.

The nesting blackbird rises, a prey just missed.

The kestrel soars up, his tail is like a fan from a Jane Austen novel about circumstance, and as he glides away from his ill-matched move, Alex's heart beats as fast as that woodpecker on the beech.

She saved the blackbird, she killed the kestrel babies, perhaps.

Alex makes it to the building door as she always does, hot and tired and well and just in time. Her head is grazed by the kestrel's claws, but she won't know it until she looks in a mirror. She is not thinking about this. She has something else to aim for - how to get more minutes with Stephen. She pants up the stairs. Already Alex is looking forward to the next day, the next run, the same day, a new day.

On the Road Again

It always starts with Cat walking in. I don't have to concentrate on this bit, don't have to go searching for the memories, they're there on the surface or just a smidge under.

'Suckers,' Cat says by way of greeting, closing the door behind her. My heart pounds, and if I could smile, I would. She looks incredible. But I calm my breathing, knowing accuracy is everything at this point. It has to be correct, the memory I mean, otherwise what's the point?

Mike looks across at her and whistles. This makes Steve glance up from his mirror, a rare event in itself especially as he's only halfway through his own make-up with one eye a livid turquoise, and the other one bare. 'Who ordered the prossie?' he laughs, though not waiting for a reaction before returning to his face.

Cat grins and looks at me. 'Too much?' she says.

'No', I say, and mean it. In fact, I don't think I've ever seen her look so good. My eyes betray everything I've taught them and take it upon themselves to sweep over her way too slowly. Her hair is punky and wild and bright pink - pink! When did she do that? - her make-up extravagant and gloriously tarty, her skinny black leather dress way too short, her tights black and her pixie boots high.

'Rock goddess or what?' she says, striding over to her guitar and lighting the joint I'd rolled and left sticking out between the strings. You'd never believe it but off the road she's all floaty summer dresses and flip-flops, but the road does something to you; it kind of exaggerates all the crazy inside you. Maybe we've all got some crazy inside us, and for some maybe too much. But that's what makes it fun, at least for now.

Turning, she blows a cloud of white smoke and says to

Steve, 'Turquoise, darling?'

He doesn't answer immediately, just continues layering and blending until both eyes are symmetrical. Then he says, 'So?' without bothering to look at her.

In that way that women say one thing all sweetness and light but mean the complete opposite, she says, 'I like it. Suits you.'

I catch Mike's eye and pull a snarly, petty, here-we-go face, and he does one back, only far more exaggerated than mine, and I cough a laugh, pick up my sticks and do a drum roll on a stack of NME magazines piled on the coffee table in front of me, finishing with an imaginary cymbal, so I have to make the 'tish' noise myself.

That's his cue. Taking a final hit before stubbing out his joint, he reaches for his base, puts it on his knee and begins plucking the strings. It's not plugged in so I can't hear it, but I can tell by the shape of his playing it's All Dolled Up, the band's second hit and our opener.

Not on the mags this time but in the air, I tap out the drum beat roughly in time to Mike's playing, knowing it will be much slicker when we get out on stage, not least because I'll be able to hear him.

Wedging the joint between her pillar-box red lips, Cat swings the guitar strap over her shoulder, the white Telecaster coming to rest in the familiar spot in front of her hips and begins playing along.

Outside the support band has thrashed out their final song, and the audience are restless for the main act. It's funny how you can hear restlessness. I try and block it out – try and fail, I don't know anyone who can – and concentrate on keeping in time. Even though we've done this a million times, we're nervous. No one says it, not directly, but like the sound of restlessness, you can also hear nerves. Anyway, this is how we loosen up. It's our routine. I know some bands who talk and talk and talk, joke about, even fight, but us, we're quiet, the odd word here and there, the odd joint, it's like we save all the energy for when we get out there. And let's face it, at our age, we can't afford to spill it backstage.

Make-up done, Steve switches to working on his hair. He can see us in reflection and hums along, taking ages longer than he used to in order to get the coiffuring right, but come on, singers and their egos, right?

For a while Steve and Cat were an item, but it was doomed from the start. The whole groupie thing, with girls coming backstage after a gig, is never conducive to a serious relationship, and so they split within a year when Steve caught Cat snogging a roadie behind the lighting rig and was livid he'd been saying no to groupie sex when she'd been at it all the time. Not that she had, she's not like that, but the road, man, the road. We all tried to tell him, but he wouldn't have it. And so the split was loud and sweary and angry and lasted for ages. That's why we haven't released a studio album for eighteen months, because they couldn't stand to be in the same space as each other. Then it just fizzled out, time probably, and things drifted back pretty much as they were before. That's when me and Cat got together, but that's top secret, although I think Mike suspects.

Two thirds of the way through the song Cat launches into her solo, her fingers flitting up and down the neck of her guitar. Out there, when we do it for real, this is the point when the crowd go mental, screaming and chanting her name. Can you imagine thirty thousand people chanting your name? Unless you're a singer or a guitarist, chances are you'd never know what that feels like. Certainly, if you're a drummer you wouldn't. A drummer's chant would be more like, 'Wos-his-name, wos-his-name, wos-his-name?' Sure, there's your Keith Moons or Cozy Powells, but for the most part, we're the unknown ones, and that suits me just fine.

I spoke to Moon a couple of months ago, bumped into him right after the Roller in the swimming pool incident, said he couldn't even remember getting in the car let alone taking it for a swim. Now that, let me tell you, is one crazy cat.

At the point when the solo comes to an end, I smash down

both sticks on an imaginary tom and look over at Mike, who picks up the beat with his base. If you think the Stones have a tight rhythm section, you'd grin yourselves a stay in a funny farm if you heard us.

There's a knock at the door and a face looks in. 'Lights down in five minutes, okay?'

My tummy does a flip-flop. It is fear, but the feeling is much bigger than just that. It's everything, like losing your virginity on Christmas day—no, it's like Christmas Eve, knowing you're going to lose your virginity tomorrow. That sense of anticipation and excitement and scared and uncertainty all wrapped up in inevitability. Delicious, in its own way.

I'm pretty sure we all feel a version of the same thing, but we're also arrogant with it and know nothing starts without us and don't even drop a beat until we reach the end of the song. Only then do we start gathering our stuff and making for the door.

Outside the hallway is flaky yellow wall paint and cold concrete floor, bright florescent lights, and a smell that makes you think of a school after everyone's gone home.

We go through several doors with me and Cat behind the other two. I feel her hand sneak into mine and squeeze, and I squeeze back. Then we're on the stage. The curtain is down, the lights back here dim, just enough for us to move about without knocking into things. I go to my kit and sit on the stool, carefully placing the sticks on the tom in front of me so they won't roll off and stretch my shoulders trying to work out the knots. Then, all the lights go out. It's pitch black. And the curtain goes up.

'Hey, wake up. Come on, it's lunch time. Wake up.'

I hear the voice, and I feel the gentle shake. Blinking, I drag myself into the now, even though I wasn't asleep.

I feel the bed moving up, pillows being plumped behind me until I'm sitting up. Clare's my carer. She's nice. I like her. When I'm in the right position, she sits on the side of the bed next to me. She's got a bowl of lukewarm soup and dips a spoon into it, then moves it to my mouth. It's tomato.

When I first came to the home, I could feed myself, but the arthritis in my hands from all the years of drumming got so bad they're useless now, so I'm fed like a baby. I know it has to be done, but still.

Clare's fun, she talks to me, and they don't all, you know. Some of them sit there and feed me in silence. But not Clare. She's twenty-two, lives with her mum since her dad left them, and has a boyfriend she thinks is cheating on her with a girl from his work. And she loves music.

Sometimes, when the owner isn't about, she wears band T-shirts. Once, she even wore one of ours. It was chicken soup that day, and I ate it staring at the face of me forty years ago. I often wonder what she would have said if she knew she was wearing me.

She shaves a dribble off my chin and pops it back into my mouth.

Truth is, I had much more fun back in the day. So that's where I spend my time, reliving old memories. That's where I'm happiest. Back with Cat and Steve and Mike. Back when we were a band, and not just any band, but a great band. They still play our music, you know. On the radio and sometimes on TV when they have those music shows from yesteryear.

I miss Cat the most. We never got married, never had kids, nothing like that. Spent too much time on the road. But we were happy, and oh man did we have some crazy fun.

The bowl's empty now and Clare tips me back down. I want to thank her, but that's another thing that doesn't work.

She touches my face gently and says, 'Go back to sleep, I'll see you for dinner,' and I think, I'm not asleep. I rarely sleep. But I close my eyes just the same. Close them to shut out the now and go back to my happy time on the road. And I'm good at it. Really good at it. The instant my eyes shut I'm back.

You can hear the curtain going up, you wouldn't think you could, but you can hear the mechanism, and then you hear nothing but the whoosh of sound from the audience as it hits you, and it is a hit; you can feel it as much as hear it.

Cat's over to the left looking at me. Steve on the right, Mike in the middle. They're all looking at me even though it's still dark. Then the spotlight turns on. Just one. One single beam of bright white light shining down on me and lighting me up like a star. Reaching for my sticks I pick them up, one in each hand, and raise them into the air, holding them up, ready. The screams from the crowd lift and lift and lift until they come together into a single, piercing sound.

Then, loud as I can, I shout, 'One, two... one, two, three, four...'

Another Pineapple

'Mandy! Go the market and buy me the biggest pineapple you can.'

Mandy hovers over the mechanical calendar on the sideboard. She is allowed to press the brass plunger just once a day when the playtime bell rings at the school next door and that is now. Her round face breaks into a ripe smile, soft cheeks pressing upward into tender blue eyes as the calendar blinks and settles on 14th May, 1981.

'Mandy! Uncle Mick gets home today. There'll be hell to pay if there's no pineapple, and he hates canned.'

Granny gasps and her face scrunches up like a paper bag in Uncle Mick's fist. She clutches her side. The clock ticks and Mandy holds her breath. Granny's eyes slowly open again.

'Now, no going to Phyllis Warren's sweetshop,' she says, sweat glistening on her face. 'And no chasing the pigeons today, understand? Straight there, straight back. He could be here by half-eleven.'

Mandy watches Granny's face as she reaches shakily for the Daily Mail.

'Who on earth would shoot him? I don't know. Anything is possible.' She looks up. 'Well, off you go!'

Mandy slams the front door, chases next door's cat across the empty street and runs towards Market Square as fast as she can against the wind, Granny's green pound note pleated in her soft hand. Her hair whips about her face. She sings to herself as she runs, anything is possible, anything is possible.

The market sucks her in: stall canopies flapping, dogs barking, shoppers chattering, stallholders shouting, pigeon wings clapping and the big flag cracking on the pole over the town hall. Past the flower man and the smelly fish van, Mandy reaches the fruit and veg stall and speaks extra clearly for the beautiful brown man who is never rude to her.

'A big pineapple, please,' she says. 'For Granny.'

The brown eyes crinkle. 'For Granny? Aah…' Long fingers lift each pineapple to his nose until he finds the right one.

'Uncle Mick is coming home today.'

The brown eyes widen, and the smile vanishes.

'Yeah? You take care now.'

Mandy grasps the pineapple as tightly as the prickles will allow and turns to watch a fat pigeon staring at her. 'Anything is possible,' she tells it and quickly ducks as a bumblebee buzzes a hair's breadth from her ear, rises and flies hard the length of the square, colliding with the window of the Teaspoon Café where Bette Murray jumps at the plunk of bee-on-glass.

Bette glances again at the red-haired woman at the window table, hunched over her third coffee, eyes alert to every movement outside. The red isn't natural. Bette huffs and polishes the last two teaspoons from the Scotland rack, a bagpiper and a Glenfinnan Tower.

The red-haired woman flinches as the town hall clock booms eleven times. She closes her eyes, rotates a zodiac ring on her finger and then looks quickly out across the market, searching the milling crowd. She drops her head, taps a cigarette from her packet and nods across to Bette for another coffee.

Bette glances out into the market and sees Nan Brewer's ungainly granddaughter chasing pigeons, a pineapple clutched in her arms. What do they call it these days? Down's syndrome. Nothing but innocence in that round face. Must be nearly eighteen now.

The round face breaks into laughter as two pigeons nearly collide in their haste to get away from her.

'You'll drop that pineapple,' an old man calls, and she puts it down on the statue steps. Now her hands are free to clap as she chases, and the fish man roars as one of her pigeons nearly flies into his van. Mandy can hear Bucks Fizz making their minds up on his radio.

The cheese man calls to her. He is the fattest man Mandy has ever seen.

'Have some cheese, lassie!' Then, 'Watch this,' he says to his brother-in-law. 'She can name any cheese on this counter. Watch.'

Mandy loves cheese. 'Mmm,' she says as the flavour swells on her tongue and fills her head.

'What is it, then?' the cheese man's brother-in-law asks with a sneer.

'Stilton.'

'Well, I never. She's right.'

The fish man watches sourly and wonders what will become of the pineapple at the foot of the old duke's statue, which is a question in Bette Murray's mind as she glances out from her café, hands busy with Goddard's polish and a soft cloth.

A fresh pineapple can mean only one thing. Mick Brewer is on his way home again. He's done a couple of years this time. Bette shivers and watches the red-haired woman rotate her ring again, eyes fixed on the square, and draw on her cigarette, sucking the smoke deep into her lungs and exhaling a long, high-tension plume. If she's kept waiting long enough, Bette may sell a lunch into the bargain.

Father Bernard hurries past the café, the cape of his cassock blowing furiously in the wind, his head bowed, his lips mid-prayer for the healing of the Holy Father. Bette offers her own prayer for Nan Brewer's health. God help her; that son and his daughter, unholy burdens, both. Poor, ailing woman.

The poor, ailing woman herself glances at her kitchen clock and swallows two painkillers. Can't let Mick see her like this. Train or bus, this time? She pictures the Platform 1 newspaper stall where she stood to meet him last time, and that is where Len Winters stands as he waits for the London train and listens to the announcement.

'The next train to arrive at Platform 1 will be the eleven

twenty-two stopping service…'

Not his, then, and he relaxes, watching the bright headlight of the eleven twenty-two grow steadily bigger and the engine finally rush into the station, braking for all it is worth. A balding man in a crumpled grey suit leaps from carriage B, runs along the platform and down the steps to the taxi rank.

'Café on Market Square!' he pants to the taxi driver, Ted. 'Missed my train. Get me there quick. Life or death.'

'Maybe the Teaspoon,' Ted replies. 'Or the West Winds.' He shrugs. 'Life or death it is.'

Eleven minutes is the quickest time in which Ted can drive from the station to the corner of Brick Street on the north side of Market Square which is, coincidentally, the exact time in which a pineapple will reach that same point, in the arms of a girl who is currently circling the statue of an ancient duke, clapping her hands, ignoring the shouts of an old man and noticing the brightness of orange flowers on the flower man's stall.

'Anything is possible, anything is possible,' she chants as she skips between irritable shoppers, pats a black Labrador and stops just short of the flower stall, never quite sure of the flower man's temper. Orange, yellow, red and pink are all bunched up together, fluttering in the wind, the flower man's voice bellowing the prices.

He pauses. 'Alright, Poppet?' But he doesn't smile. Pigeons on top of his stall bow solemnly to each other before flying off one, two, three, across the square and down to the statue steps where a pineapple, just like Mandy's, sits alone until she remembers, runs back to it and hugs it as she skips, skirt flying in the wind.

She trips.

'There, now!' says the cross old man as Mandy gets up. She pouts at the blood on her knee until she sees that money has fallen out of her pocket, perhaps enough for pear drops. She can already feel the roughness of their sugar on her tongue.

The red-haired woman watches her from the window of the

café, the zodiac ring rotating. The town hall clock plays the Westminster chimes again, the first two lines.

Fury rips through her. He's not coming. Even now she hesitates. A pigeon lands on the statue and takes off again. She'll watch for a pigeon to land on the statue just three more times and then she'll go, just leave and forget. Hands shaking, she drinks the dregs of her coffee. The first pigeon lands, and she swallows hard. She has been so sure he would come. If only she could have seen him once more, anything could have been possible.

The pigeon takes off and circles, swoops down behind the knitwear stall and rises again, climbs and dives towards an old man on a bench but is wind-buffeted away and comes to rest on the statue again. The second landing. The red-haired woman grips her bag and swivels her knees free of the table, ears straining for the long-awaited footsteps on the pavement.

The pigeon turns, watches Market Square and then tips as a gust of wind sends it off balance. It circles over the town hall, above converging movement: a car rushing towards the market from behind the town hall and a large girl hurtling northward towards her favourite sweet shop. The pigeon glides, the taxi driver turns his head to speak over his shoulder and the girl's legs pound. Closer and closer. The pigeon drifts down towards the head of the statue. And lands.

The red-haired woman sobs, bolts out of the door and runs across the street into the square, ignoring the squeal of the taxi's brakes as it slews towards her, and equally heedless of the pineapple and the girl who dashes across the road ten yards away. The crumpled grey suit spills out of the taxi and hurls itself into the market calling, 'Sheila!'

The pineapple disappears down Brick Street, towards the pink shop-front belonging to Phyllis Warren.

'What a beautiful pineapple,' Phyllis cries. Another pineapple. Mick must be out again.

'Uncle Mick is coming home today,' Mandy says. 'Can I have some pear drops? Is this enough money?'

Uncle! How long will they persist with that lie?

'And have you said a prayer for the Pope?' she asks Mandy.

'Why?'

'Why? Because some wicked person has shot him.'

'Does that hurt?' Mandy asks, grasping her side like Granny does, and Phyllis does not miss the action, though what will become of the girl if Nan Brewer does not pull through...

'Yes, it hurts,' Phyllis says more gently and sees a sheet of newspaper blow past the window, curling and spinning in a gust of wind that carries it to the end of Brick Street and across to the back of the knitwear stall, catching the eye of Bette Murray as she stands at her café window watching a man in a crumpled grey suit plead with her red-haired customer at the foot of the duke's statue.

Ted, the taxi man, asks for coffee.

'Might as well,' he says. 'Hasn't paid his fare yet. They may need a ride back to the station.'

He picks up a newspaper and carries it to the window table where he quietly pockets an abandoned packet of cigarettes and turns to the back page, which is the page that Mick Brewer is reading as his bus reaches its terminus in Market Square.

Same old market, Mick thinks a few moments later; same bloody pigeons. He must be mad to come back here.

Some bloke in a grey suit is yanking the arm of an angry red-head by the statue, and as Mick walks south he catches sight of Mandy dashing homeward with a large pineapple, the sight of which makes Mick's mouth water.

He follows her slowly, inhaling the familiar fishy stench of Bennett's van before turning down Mum's street and aiming a kick at next door's cat.

The door is open, and Nan Brewer waits for her son. She breathes the smell of institution as he throws his tatty jacket over a chair. He looks older, harder. Mandy grasps the pineapple and watches him warily. Mick gives her a dismissive scowl.

'Anything is possible,' Mandy whispers to Granny.

139

Granny glances at her in surprise as she takes the pineapple from her. She smiles wearily.

'Yes, I suppose so, love. Anything is possible.'

Both at Once

Ahlam does the washing up. Same as every morning. Fouad is at work and the kids are at school. This is the bit of her day when she enjoys the quiet, the bit before it becomes oppressive. Her kitchen is at the front of the house, so the window above the sink looks out onto the street. Ahlam has learned that this is unusual. Most British homes have the kitchen at the back and a front room at, well, the front. But she prefers it this way. It means she can keep an eye on the children playing in the garden while she sits on the sofa struggling to read one of their English storybooks. And it means she can watch the comings and goings outside while she does the dishes. She watches the golden women of her street. The women whose feet do not seem to touch the ground.

Opposite live the Bihar family. They are at once different and the same. The rest of the neighbourhood is filled with white families, as is all of Hinchley Wood. All of Surrey it seems, though in truth Ahlam has not seen much of it. Fouad says there are rough parts, dangerous parts, even here in Surrey. She does not believe him. Ahlam knows real danger. She has been close enough to danger to see its nostrils flare. It does not live in Surrey. Ahlam picks up the book she is meant to read today but puts it down again. She cannot muster the will to care about Jack or his beanstalk. In Arabic she has read Plato and Marx, for goodness sake. She turns the radio to Al Jazeera.

The Bihars come out of their front door while Ahlam is drying her hands. There are three of them. Vikram, a rotund accountant, who Ahlam is sure sees a different reflection in the mirror. He slicks the few hairs across his bald head in a way that makes her slightly nauseous. He always uses a convoluted vocabulary she struggles to follow. Fouad says this is his attempt to fit in, but he sounds like nobody else on the street. According to Vikram, everyone is a bugger of some kind: crafty, sneaky, charming. Ahlam looked the word up in her dictionary and found even less reason for its frequent use. His wife, Sangeeta, does fit. She wears the same quilted vests and tall boots as the golden women. She often leaves her house with a yoga mat under her arm, which Ahlam mistook for a prayer mat the first time she saw it. When the golden women smile at Ahlam there is pity in their eyes, but Sangeeta smiles only with irritation. The little boy is adorable, though. Same age as Shareef. They play together sometimes, which Ahlam is sure tightens Sangeeta's smile even further.

Sangeeta is wearing very high heels and a baby pink two-piece suit. Not a good shade for her, and the skirt is much too short. Anything above the ankles is too short for Ahlam. Not that she is particularly conservative, no, she just does not think anyone needs to see her chunky calves. Vikram fiddles with his tie and Sangeeta slaps his hands away. She does the same to the boy. They climb into their green Range Rover. Moss green, Sangeeta had called it. Ahlam wonders if this is some kind of mould. Vikram starts the engine, and they disappear towards the A3.

Ahlam makes a glass of black tea with lots of sugar. As she sips, the sounds of Aleppo come back. First, it is the sound of Leila's rooster, next the endless street hawkers sing-shouting their wares. She likes that. But then it is the terrifying noises of the recent past. Noises that are barely human yet all too human. Something hammers at her skull, and her knees start to wobble. She switches the radio to music, sits, and tries to resist the Jaffa Cakes.

On her darker days, when Ahlam forces herself to write down the things she is grateful to England for, the list usually goes: an absence of guns, an abundance of daffodils, and Jaffa Cakes. The nice lady from the Home Office, who came to interview them, had introduced Ahlam to these orangey delights. She said that there is a major debate amongst the English as to whether they are cakes or just biscuits. After she left, Ahlam and Fouad laughed until tears ran down their faces. The things these English argue about. Too much time on their hands.

Now Ahlam has nothing but time. Time she spends reading kiddies' books, criticising her neighbours' clothes, and remembering. Her nails dig into the kitchen table.

She eats a Jaffa Cake over the sink to avoid crumbs. Perhaps if she eats enough of these, if she starts taking her tea with milk, it will make up for her lack of a yoga mat. She will never wear those rubber boots though, never. No matter how muddy it gets. As she finishes a second cake, she notices a blonde girl walking along the street. The child seems no older than ten and yet she is alone. She is not from around here. Ahlam is sure she would have noticed this girl at the school – that hair is hard to miss, and no Hinchey Wood mother would dress their daughter in such a dated dress. More tablecloth than dress, in fact. The girl walks confidently, with focus. When she reaches the Bihars' driveway she stops, looks over both shoulders, then walks up to the door and lets herself in.

Excitement jangles through Ahlam. How could Vikram have forgotten to lock the door? What could a little white girl be doing in there alone? She may not even be safe. Ahlam has been inside before and knows the place is full of statues of multi-armed Hindu gods, fingers pointing in all directions. The child could lose an eye. Ahlam pulls a purple hijab over her hair and squeezes her feet into sparkly slippers. In the name of God, the Most Gracious, the Most Merciful. She steps outside and crosses the street.

When she tries the Bihars' door it is locked. Ahlam stands in the flowerbed peering through a window. The girl is sitting at the kitchen table. Sangeeta has failed to tidy up after breakfast and their bowls litter the table. From what Ahlam can see, it looks like they had dal. The girl picks up a spoon to taste. She screws up her mouth, the spices clearly not appealing at this time of the morning. Ahlam chuckles. What was she expecting?

The girl disappears towards the lounge. Ahlam hurries to the side gate, picking up the key from under a fake rock, as she has seen Vikram do so many times. She creeps into the back garden. There is an empty bottle of wine on the patio table. Ahlam tuts. She cranes her neck to look through the bi-fold doors. There is the girl reclining in Vikram's leather chair. She looks like she owns it. She shifts a little, turns down her lips and moves to the sofa. Still she seems displeased. The girl is motionless for a moment then jumps off and runs up the stairs, knocking over an elephant deity as she passes.

She needs help. She is not right in the head. Ahlam pushes at the handle and the door slides open. There must be a mother or medical professional or someone somewhere frantically searching for this girl right now. Ahlam enters the house.

Whenever she sees the Bihars in public, they are trying to appear as English as possible – the clothes, the words, the little boy's name that she cannot now remember. But here in their home it is pure India. The pictures, the colours, even the smell of the place. Ahlam cannot understand how you do this. How you live two parallel lives. Or why. Is this a price England expects her to pay?

Ahlam looks around the lounge. She picks up a magazine. The lady on the front has flawless skin and pomegranate lips. Inside there are pictures of the Princess. The one people love, not the halfie-halfie one. Sangeeta has circled a picture of a cheaper version of the skirt the Princess is wearing. This one might actually suit her. Ahlam walks towards the staircase.

With every step she climbs, something presses down on her more firmly. Her shoulders slump, but she cannot give up now. She looks first in the boy's room. The duvet and pillows are thrown to the floor, and his poster of a football team that wears blue is ripped. The room is empty. She walks across the landing and steps into the master bedroom. Here is the girl. She is partially under the covers but sitting up and brushing her hair.

They stare at each other in silence for a moment, the brush moving to a regular beat up and down, up and down.

'What you do here?' Ahlam asks. Embarrassment at her own accent reddens her cheeks. The girl says nothing.

'What you do here?' Ahlam repeats. 'I help. Tell me.'

Darkness flashes across the girl's face, and she flings off the duvet. She is fully clothed and still wearing her shoes. She runs up to Ahlam screaming, 'What are you doing here?' She pushes Ahlam hard against the wall and sprints down the stairs.

Ahlam stares into the mirror. Her breathing is hard and shallow. What is she doing here? This is not how it is meant to be. The bedroom is a mess. She picks the duvet off the floor, tears shimmering in her eyes. She opens and closes drawers at random. Then she sees it.

The bottle of Vikram's cologne is beside the sink in the ensuite. Drakkar Noir. He always uses too much of it; it almost makes Ahlam's eyes water. Her brother Salim wears the same thing.

Wore.

Before.

War.

She sprays some on her wrist. She inhales deeply and holds her breath for as long as she can. She kicks off her slippers and slides under the bedcovers. Ahlam sprays more cologne onto a pillow and pulls it over her face. She presses it down hard, harder. In the blackness, Salim floats towards her. In the blackness, she sees her children drifting away. In the blackness, she wants to deserve to be here.

She must have fallen asleep. The pillow is lifted from Ahlam's face, and her eyes meet Sangeeta's. Vikram and the little boy are peering in from the doorway. The boy is holding the broken elephant god. Ganesh. The elephant god is called Ganesh. Avi, her favourite tailor back home, had the same one on his counter. The god of beginnings, the remover of obstacles. Ahlam smiles as she remembers this. Sangeeta's face softens, and she puts a hand on Ahlam's shoulder.

At the kitchen table, Sangeeta slides away the bowls and puts a cup of tea in front of Ahlam.

'I added ginger. I hope that's alright,' she says. 'I've never understood why the British put cow juice in tea.' She looks out the window as she adds, 'Anyway, I'm lactose intolerant.' Ahlam drinks in silence. The fire of the ginger feels good in her throat. 'You've been in here before, haven't you?' Ahlam nods and holds up two fingers. Sangeeta looks out the window again. 'Why?'

Ahlam wants to tell her. She wants to tell her what she saw and did not see. She wants to tell her that she is here and not here. She wants to tell her that forward and backward are the same thing, and only by holding on to the frayed edges of both can she keep herself from disappearing. But she does not have the words.

'For understand,' she says.

Sangeeta nods and sits down opposite her.

'Yes,' she says, blowing ginger scented steam across the table. 'Yes, I see.'

The Skirt

Where are you going?

He lifted his head at her movement from the sofa.

'Cup of tea.'

He was watching her as she carried on moving. She didn't turn, but aimed herself at the kitchen door. Her skirt whispered to her as she moved. Bias cut, with a pattern of stylised fern. 'An African print, called Aya,' the sales assistant had said, and she had put her hand to her heart. It was so long since she had looked someone - a stranger - in the eye. He wouldn't know she had smiled and had looked at the woman. But he knew she had bought a skirt unsupervised.

'Would you like one too?' Bright voice.

The telly flickered on mute; a rare falcon watching from across the Five Great Mountains. She went to the kitchen. His silence followed her. The butter knife was lying on its side. She could imagine it in her hand, the gentle slope of its bone handle.

Teas: Yarrow, Sage, Zinnia, Thyme and Chamomile.

You really need to get help he had said yesterday. Her hair was coming out in clumps on the pillow. Psychiatrist or something.

Her skirt was an embrace around her. Perhaps the women who had made it had pressed their hands to it, had held it to their faces in blessing, before sending it to be cut into shape to cover someone just like her.

'You made me jump!'

He was right there in the doorway.

Now her fingers went to the fresh thyme, pressed - and there was that fine-edged scent coming up to meet her.

'Aya,' she murmured to herself.

'It means defiance in my culture,' whispered the salesclerk, handing the shopping bag over.

His shimmering anger was like sound waves, blasting through all air till it hit her.

His jaw pulled the drawstring knotted in her stomach - if she backed away it would get tighter, so she stepped forward an inch.

'Builders' tea?'

On the screen through the doorway the falcon took flight.

The Ice Cream Man

We called him the Ice Cream Man. He drove a white truck through the neighborhoods on Mondays and Wednesdays and laughed when he saw us chasing him. He wore a white suit and a funny white hat with a short bill like an umpire's cap, and we called him the Ice Cream Man.

He came when balmy days turned feverish and sweaty, and his tinkling music floated through the air like the sound of ice crackling in a cool drink. Our mothers would go to their purses, handing out dimes and quarters to our urgent entreaties, telling us to hurry before the Ice Cream Man got away. Then off we'd spring, delighted in the chase, our eyes wide in the half fear that our prey would escape, the music fading away before our running feet; down one block and then another we'd run, calling out anxiously to each other, then cutting across a neighbor's lawn and putting on a final burst of speed as the white truck came into sight, the music seeming to swell as if he were just about to leave. We'd pound up to the truck with labored breaths, and he'd stand in the doorway, tall and cool, surveying us with amusement and disdain.

'What's this?' he'd ask of the outstretched hands and clamour. Half a dozen voices would rise in answer, each shoving the other to higher decibels, all seeking his attention.

'Ice cream?' he'd ask and scratch his head. 'You don't want me. You want the Ice Cream Man.'

The voices would cry out then, not in unison but in six or seven part harmony. 'But you ARE the Ice Cream Man!'

Then he'd hit his head with the flat palm of his hand and roll his eyes apologizing that of course we were right. More questions, obtuse and full of fun, driving us more frantic until finally he'd relent and Fudgesicles and Dream DeLites,

Sidewalk Sundaes and Frozen Surprises were handed out. Always he seemed to hear the weakest voice first handing out the icy treasure to that small fist first, he or she looking up happily, before popping the dripping coolness into their mouth.

When all the supplicants had been satisfied, we milled around the truck, reluctant to let him go. Some would ask why he was an ice cream man, and how did he keep the ice cream cold. He'd do a quick two-step and make up silly rhymes, almost falling, then hold his nose at the bad jokes he made. He never stayed long, a minute or two before shooing us away in mock horror that he was so late, scattering us like blown-upon lady bugs.

He'd wave as we retreated, legs thrashing before turning to yell goodbyes. Once when I stopped and turned, I saw him wave and smile a sad kind of ice cream smile before he turned on the music and drove round the corner.

We often played in the park that summer. Meeting and arguing, friendships made and broken one day to be remade the next. We played a lot of softball when Bennie Johnson remembered his bat and ball. The rules were altered as often as the players, but as the summer began to close, we settled down to play every day, filling vacant positions with little brothers or girls who didn't cry. Sometimes I'd see the Ice Cream Man drive by in his white truck, pausing for a moment or two, his music silent, then slowly continuing on his way.

Our games were noisy and disorganized, frequently interrupted by shrill arguments of safe or out, both sides vehement in their certainty. Finally, the cause was resolved by the need to continue before parents called us home; the dispute ending as quickly as it began except for the lone voice whose case had been lost in the back-lot court of justice.

The first time the Ice Cream Man stopped his truck near the field, the ball game broke up as the two sides refused to borrow or give or agree to share, then shouting, ran up to the truck. He'd shaken his head then and said he wasn't the Ice Cream

Man that day. He had on regular clothes and wasn't wearing his white cap. He invited us to look in his truck, and only when each inquisitor's curiosity was satisfied, did we give up our prey and wander back to the field.

'What're you doin' here then?' I asked.

The Ice Cream Man paused at the question, looking off toward the baseball field where the others were already tossing the ball around, yelling and screaming. 'Remembering,' he said with a sad ice cream smile, 'just remembering,' then told me to hurry, I was holding up the game. I reluctantly left; a dozen questions left unanswered at the prodding of the first.

We came to expect him every afternoon on Tuesdays and Thursdays, and once when Bennie showed up and told us he'd lost his softball, we wandered aimlessly over to the Ice Cream Man's truck, telling him about our bad luck; there would be no ball game that day. The Ice Cream Man only laughed and did a little tap dance, bringing out, magically, a softball, totally new, a gleaming white jewel.

'Bring it back,' he said, as we rushed off.

When the game was over, everyone came to the truck, and we solemnly handed the ball back. Already the first scratches and darkened patches showed on the surface. The Ice Cream Man examined the ball minutely then laughed, throwing the ball in the air, telling us how well we'd played. Then he tossed the ball to Tommy Bentson, the youngest and poorest player. Tommy beamed and asked if it was really his.

'For sure it is,' the Ice Cream Man said in an Irish brogue. 'And the captain of the team from now on you'll be.' And so it was; Tommy choosing his side carefully from then on. Tommy made All State in baseball his last year in high school, but by then he'd probably forgotten about the Ice Cream Man. Or maybe not.

As the prospect of school became an oppressive reality, we started ending our games early to go over to talk with the Ice Cream Man. He'd sit on the steps of his white truck and remember every one's name and important events. He'd joke about Timmy Smith being an old man on his tenth birthday and how amazing it was for Linda to be so pretty, and so good at third base too. I remember she blushed at that, and the older boys stared at her for a moment.

Afterwards he'd call, 'All aboard!' and we'd ride to the other side of the park where we could cut across home. 'All ashore that don't want to be taken home and made into Popsicles.' The younger ones shook their heads shyly, while the older ones said, 'No way!' then everyone would jump off, yelling their goodbyes. He'd watch us running off, always smiling his ice cream smile.

Just before school started, the Ice Cream Man stopped coming by. We missed him in the rush and pomp of a new year, the shuffle of before school sales, of new shoes and bargain shirts. Sometimes we wondered about the Ice Cream Man and what he did in the winter. Tommy thought he probably went north to help Santa Claus make more ice cream, but no one took him seriously.

Later though, as the winter in all its dreariness drove us inside, the Ice Cream Man became for us, a secret agent disguised to escape unjust punishment or dreadful evil. He was perhaps a mountain climber, or hero, so wronged by evil that he sought revenge in as many forms as our imaginations. It became a standing rule no one could play the Ice Cream Man twice in a row, and each of us had to play benign spectators or vile bad guys before he or she could again be our hero.

The pupae stages of winter passed, discarded like an empty skin in the summer warmth. The last class bell rang, releasing us into the fragile freedom of our mayfly summer.

We waited eagerly for the Ice Cream Man's return and hoped he had not changed and would remember us. The first sounds of the music box jingle of the ice cream truck pulsed in the summer heat, tinkling the recesses of our memories as we raced unheeding to see the legend and forgotten friend. No one had stopped to gather money, the ice cream second to the man. The white truck stopped as we hurtled up to it, and a dark-haired man, a stranger, looked down at us. The Ice Cream Man was gone. When the man found we had no money, he brusquely started up the truck and was gone. Later, when he came again, we looked for any kind of ice cream smile or joke. He only counted back the change as if an auditor were grading his every move.

The Ice Cream Man had been swallowed into oblivion like so much else of our childhood that had seemed worthwhile and warm.

It was a few years later that I learned what had happened. Someone's mother had called up the ice cream company and complained about the strangeness of one of their employees. It had not seemed difficult then for us to trust him or believe that he could be what he seemed. Yet now it is easy to know the fears and hauntings of the world we make and live in.

The ice cream trucks are all gone now, replaced by convenience stores and Wal Mart foil packaging. They say that memories are short lived, and now I am afraid of getting old. I find myself reaching back to those days of ice cream trucks and warm short summers, often taking walks to nowhere in particular, watching the neighborhood children playing, sometimes even leaning on a flimsy outfield fence to watch the stumbling marvel of a pick-up softball game.

Once the center-fielder, a skinny kid like Tommy Bentson used to be, fielded a fungo and after throwing the ball back to the infield, eyed me with suspicion and dislike, his voice echoing from my past, 'Hey, what're ya doing here?'

I looked at him for a moment, pausing. 'Remembering,' I said, with a sad ice cream smile, 'just remembering.'

The Welsh Hill Farm

There were no straight lines on the Welsh hillsides, and she knew somehow this landscape was never going to console her. The hedgerows kinked and looped, stunted trees leaned over the tracks on the hills, and there seemed no rhythm, no pattern for her to lock on to. She had grown up with small valleys punctuated by villages sewn together by fields, farms and hamlets hemmed by generations of farmers and woodsmen. But here, on the steep hillsides, the rush of water ran all year, so the farmers and their families couldn't hear the roar anymore.

But she heard the roar when she climbed up the hillside and saw the ravens skydiving, and heard the silken rustle of their wings when they flew close. For the hill above their tiny farmhouse belonged to the ravens really, it certainly belonged to no human, in spite of Eddie showing her the deeds; setting out his plans for new barns, an electricity pump attached to the waterfall, a new tractor, which she could see was too big for the tracks about the farm and too heavy for the steep slopes of the upper fields.

The hills here were huge and reached up so high she felt the earth tilt when she looked up at them. Bracken swarmed across the tops, unbroken by improbable walls or abandoned tracks, only scattered with huge rocks that looked like some giant had thrown them onto the hillside in a fit of pique. In an almost level straight line the bracken stopped, and below it struggled a seam of greyish heather that looked lifeless and crusted now, but she soon learnt it was home to a thousand sky larks in the spring. At home in the past it took very little to nudge her to pull on her boots, a whistle to next door's dog, and she would walk for hours, the movement of her body and pacing of her feet calming her. There she had climbed stiles, squeezed through gaps, admired the shining flanks of curious heifers clustered around her, pushed open rotting gates and followed paths signed and unsigned until, always, she felt better. But here there were no signposts, and the hills guarded themselves with faint paths and emptiness.

Eddie's dreams were all tied up with this farm; he didn't just breathe here, he drank in the air. He climbed up high whenever he could, until he was way above her, looking down, waving, throwing out his glee into the never flagging winds that whistled in, day and night from the west and, more often than not, brought rain. She had been caught up too, in the altitude and the stark untouched roll of grass on rock. Newly married, she had slipped from their warm bed and explored, walking out into a space wholly unlined by roads on the old Ordnance Survey map which hung on their kitchen wall, a blank nothingness marked only by three tufts of short lines warning of bogs. Empty and flat right at the top, it was indeed wet in patches marked by vivid green grass and she was surprised to find in the middle of all that emptiness, a huge, sloping, dark rock painted in large white letters with 'Elvis lives'. She had thought that day as she turned 360 degrees and saw the horizon on every side that she could carve out a life, raise children perhaps, away from the hustle, away from the crowds and the pushing.

But farming here was tough. It had been even tougher for the centuries before tractors, before wellington boots, when mud reached your knees in the winter and smelt all summer long, when there were no vets, just neighbours with homemade cures, and death was a constant companion. The vestiges of this still remained; she came to dread the slow walk through sucking black mud to feed the sheep, the desperation of their winter hunger, the bones picked by the huge red kites on the hills that were the only clues to the death of ewe after ewe. Then there were the carrion crows that waited in the spring for the sheep in labour, to peck out their eyes while helpless and beached.

But she had born Eddie two children, cooked and cleaned and become as much of a countrywoman as she could be. He had grown quieter, more determined, and then quieter still until they all tiptoed around him.

The neighbours had been reserved but kind when they first came, little eye contact, very occasional offers of advice but largely sceptical and self-contained. They nodded when Eddie told them his plans and had little to comment. But she saw them listening to his English accent and wondering why he wore an old leather gilet like their grandfathers had discarded years ago for sturdy waterproofs that kept out the incessant Welsh rain. She knew they thought Eddie foolish, a dreamer, but they kept this to themselves. Border folk do that. Friendly but distant, used to incomers but watchful, expectant of a rolling curve of enthusiasm, knockbacks and defeat, and then the 'farm for sale' signs.

Eddie was determined not to be one of those, but the same challenges hit him as those who had been here before. His flock caught something, the vet shook his head, only a handful of lambs survived that year. When she drove to the shops, almost five miles down narrow, waterlogged lanes, the shops remained bare of pasta or salad leaves, but offered numerous root vegetables and rows of tins like an army on parade. She saw their gaze behind their smiles, rimmed with pity, empty of curiosity, just a faint and wistful sadness.

She made one friend, a farmer's wife who had lived away before coming back and so was more open to newcomers. But even that friendship was guarded, stilted. It met stumbling blocks, like when she found her new friend did not have a passport and never had. She had allowed the surprise to show on her face briefly before realising she had no right to be shocked. None of the locals felt the need to leave; they did not even go away on holiday. The coast for the day in summer was their ideal holiday. Back in time to feed the stock.

So, when Eddie left early one morning without warning, packed a small case and took the car, she was unsure who to tell, who to turn to. There were nearly two hundred sheep on the hill and over twenty head of cattle knee-deep in mud below the house that needed feeding. She pulled on her boots and began. It took all day to do what Eddie did in half a day. The children made their own lunch.

The next day she did it all again, but this time the tears came, and she struggled to see while she dumped hay on the hillside and slid back down through the hail. Later that week, after dark one evening, there was a thumping on the door. Few visitors came all the way up to their farm, up the bumping track whose stones tried to slither down the hill each winter. Her heart filled her mouth. It was three neighbours, all men, some bent, some broad, all ragged in tweed jackets tied at the waist with bailer twine, the uniform of the hills, with weather-gouged faces. None of them looked directly at her. They had been talking; they had heard Eddie had gone. They had divvied up her chores, and four of them were fine to take over; one said he would take the cattle to his farm where it wasn't so wet, they'd do better there. He'd sell them for her in the first spring market. The others would feed her sheep, crossing over from the topside of the hill where their farm bordered hers.

She did not know what to say, but they did not seem to expect any words. It was sorted, they just wanted her to know.

For the next few days, every time she left the house, there was someone collecting feed or moving sheep, mending a gate or fiddling with the tractor. They were unfailingly polite but kept on doing what they were doing. On the next Sunday, she and the children sat huddled on the sofa watching a film. She had lost her appetite but knew she needed to feed the children who had lived all week on sandwiches, tinned soup and baked potatoes. But she couldn't face the thought of feeding anything anymore.

She thought she heard something and went to the door, leaving the two children on the sofa, eyes glued to the screen.

There was no one there. But as she went to close the door, she saw a tray on the doorstep. It was a Sunday roast, plated up, with the gravy in an eggcup covered tightly with cling-film.

All that winter and into the spring, some kind of Sunday roast was left each week on her doorstep. The quality of the meat and vegetables varied greatly; they must all have divvied up this task too, but the kindness was the same each and every Sunday.

The Girl Dancing the Tarantella

The road leading up to Monte Sant'Angelo is long and dusty. It is lined by a dry-stone wall to the north and a single row of cypress trees to the south. The sun is at its highest point in the sky, so the shadows cast by the trees are too short to provide shade for the travellers below.

The procession is as follows.

First, a man riding a horse. A boy walks beside him.

Next, several more men, some travelling on horses, others on foot.

Next, three hundred Gentile di Puglia, a breed of sheep indigenous to Southern Italy, stretching out of sight like a grey river.

Last, several more men, checking for stragglers who have wandered away from the herd.

The heads of the sheep bob up and down as they walk up the hill. Some of the flock sport large impressive horns, others short perky ears. They will spend the summer grazing on the pastures of Monte Gargano.

The man at the front of the group rides a large black horse. The boy beside him wears loose clothing made from white linen with a leather satchel slung over his shoulder. He holds a wooden cane in his right hand and a hat in his left hand which is brown and tapers towards a point on the crown. The sunlight shimmers off the sweat clinging to his face and neck. He sweeps his damp fringe out of his eyes.

'Why do we have hair instead of wool?' he says.

'You're too old to ask questions like that,' the man says.

They travel in silence. Even in the spring months, heat can be seen shimmering off the path. The boy kicks out at a stone. It shoots across the ground and spins into the yellow grass by

159

the side of the track.

'You'll scare the animals,' the man says.

His beard is thick and grey, and his eyes gleam like black marbles from under the shadow cast by his hat across his face. The boy says nothing.

'Put your hat on,' the man says.

'I don't want to.'

'Your skin will burn.'

'It won't.'

'You're humiliating yourself.'

'You mean I'm humiliating you.'

'You're humiliating yourself.'

Shouts can be heard in the distance. A group of children have spotted them and are running away up the hill.

'We are nearly at Monte Sant'Angelo,' the man says.

The road levels out and limestone houses appear on the horizon glistening like white pearls. Olive farmers stand at the edge of their groves to watch them pass. The sound of music floats on the breeze from town. The people have always celebrated the transumanza. There are no gates to welcome them into Monte Sant'Angelo. Buildings simply pop up to the left and right of the road. The sheep are silent apart from the bells rattling around their necks. They pass the grand old Santuario di San Michele Arcangelo and follow the twisting streets below an arch between the houses. People shout greetings from above, their laundry floating like ghosts from the lines stretched between the balconies. A crowd has formed along the edges of the town's main avenue. It feels like everyone has gathered to watch the parade: serious men dressed in white religious gowns, children with bright eyes and grubby faces, grandmothers with deep trench-like wrinkles and gentle smiles. The man sits a little taller on his horse. They reach the stretch of road where the crowd is densest and the music loudest. The steamy aroma of marinara hangs heavy in the air. The crowd has parted to allow space for three girls to dance. They wear white lace blouses with corsets and billowing red

160

skirts. An elderly man leans against an old cart playing the accordion. He taps his foot as the girls skip across the cobbled stone.

'They are performing the tarantella,' the man says to the boy.

The boy does not hear him. He watches as the girls swirl through the thick air. They kick their feet and spin on the spot. Two of the girls hold castanets which they clap in time. The other girl holds a tambourine, shaking the bells without ever beating its surface. The boy's eyes linger on her. She has a scarlet rose in her hair and a beauty spot above her right cheek. She moves with the erratic beauty of a flickering candle. He thinks he has caught her eye, but she looks through him as he passes. She springs towards another girl and swaps her tambourine for the castanets. He can no longer walk forward and watch her dance. He turns his neck to look ahead and then up towards the man.

'Do we stop in town?'

'The slopes are only a few hours away,' the man says.

The sound of the accordion is already more distant. The boy turns back but the crowd now blocks his view. She is already a memory.

'I think we should stop here,' he says.

The man has turned to face a group standing outside a bistro. They cry ipastori and raise their glasses towards him. He acknowledges them with a nod.

'Do you hear me?' the boy says.

'I hear you.'

'And?'

'And what?'

'I think we should stop.'

'We never stop in Monte Sant'Angelo.'

'Why?'

The man says nothing. The crowd thins as they move away from the centre of town. They are soon back amongst the twisting residential streets. The boy can still picture her moving through the warm air, still hear the blaring of the accordion, still feel the mood of the crowd tingle on his skin.

'I don't want to go,' he cries.

The man looks down at him. The boy has turned his head to hide his face.

'You are too old to cry,' the man says, glancing over his shoulder at the other men.

'I don't want to go,' the boy says again.

'I know.'

'I'll never want to go.'

'You don't have a choice.'

'Why?'

'Sometimes in life we don't have a choice.'

'We always have a choice.'

'No, we don't.'

The sun beats down on them as the houses start to thin away. Beyond the last remaining buildings, a valley sweeps down towards the sea. The man adjusts his hat to protect his face.

'We could have stopped in town,' the boy says.

'We couldn't,' the man says.

'You just didn't want to.'

'We needed to get the animals through the streets as quickly as possible. We have a responsibility to the people of the town.'

The boy says nothing. The sun is hot on his skin. He places his hat on his head.

'I know their mother,' the man says.

'What?'

'I know their mother.'

'What are you talking about?'

'Her name is Carlotta Camporesi. Those were her daughters dancing the tarantella.'

'I don't know what you mean.'

The man says nothing.

'I don't,' the boy says again.

'I will introduce you to Carlotta and her daughters on the

162

journey home,' the man says.

'I thought we couldn't stop in town.'

'Your brother will be ready to lead by then.'

'I don't know what you're talking about.'

'I was your age once.'

'I don't know what you're talking about.'

There is no trace of the town now. A sheer mountain face rises to their left, and the olive groves roll down the valley to their right. The air is still, apart from the bells around the necks of the sheep and the heavy footsteps of the horses.

'We will turn off this road soon,' the man says.

'Five months is a long time,' the boy says.

'It isn't.'

'It is.'

The boy looks up at the man. He stares down the valley towards the point where the sea touches the sky.

'One day you'll realise it isn't,' he says.

The boy looks down at his boots. His feet are sore from days of walking. A layer of orange dust has seeped into the brown leather. He does not believe the man.

What If?

As she enters the water, the man the other side of the rope, in the next lane, is thrashing up and down, his rubber-encased head, a wet bullet; she hopes he will soon exhaust himself. She can never properly relax if there is anyone else in the pool. She tries to pick a quiet time and favours early evening, towards the close of day. She could have swum indoors in the relative warmth and comfort of the internal pool, but she hates the chlorinated fug that hangs over the water, the press of people, and having to navigate their flailing bodies.

Outside, the air sharp with cold, turns her breath to dry ice and her feet numb, but she wouldn't swap. The outdoor pool is an afterthought, tacked on to the side of the main building. Above her, on an upper floor through a great expanse of glass, she can see ranks of sweaty people going nowhere fast on bikes and treadmills. The pool sits next to a carpark that services a busy supermarket surrounded by an ugly open-slatted fence, through which car headlights strafe, and where from ground level she can see staccato flashes of people's legs.

Today there is a minus-something chill factor, and the wind is whipping sideways across the surface of the water in choppy wavelets; it gives off a spray that freezes the side of her face as she turns her head to breathe. Having come late to the water, she is slow and lacks any real technique, but lack of skill does not detract from her passion for swimming outside.

The bullet-headed young man ignores the steps and instead leaps out of the water on to the side of the pool in a single, suave manoeuvre, using only one hand; with the other, he simultaneously picks up his water-bottle. As the door to the indoor pool clangs shut behind him, the woman feels the soft exhilaration of coming solitude.

Left to herself she rolls onto her back, a secret ritual that initiates a loosening of perception, the precursor to deep, reflective thought. The dun grey, urban surroundings have become suffused with muted colour, the sky, an intense royal blue, flushes even deeper at the prospect of the coming night. She rolls back on to her front and, without an audience, swims easily, almost well. Soon her body slackens, and her mind slows until thoughts merge like the mixing of paint. She is no longer counts lengths as soon, unrelated, wonderful musings begin to pair-off to form ideas. This is what she has come for.

But then the door to the indoor pool clangs again, its aftershock fracturing the sound-sensitive limbo of her meditation. It is only one of the leisure complex staff sneaking out through a gate in the fence for a quick smoke, but he leaves the gate and leaning against it blows smoke rings in the dark. The black hole of the open gate leaves the woman exposed, vulnerable to the literal stares of passers-by and to some other, unnamed thing.

Soon the member of staff, perhaps not wanting to linger in the freezing air, clangs back through the door leaving an acrid, nicotine after-scent that permeates the steam above the water. She tries rolling on her back again to encourage the return of her precious equilibrium, but it's not working. And then, when she looks up at the sky punctured by the tops of trees, their feathery branches fanning the disc of a rose-gold moon no longer seem decorative. In the fast-approaching darkness, all at once, everything is jarring, alien.

She presses on, struggling to place a tantalising memory, triggered by the smoke, and retrieves it from Paris, where her sixteen-year-old self, spent a first trip away from home. This memory opens out into a series of Origami folds, each containing another expanding sensory memory. There is the first hit of a low-lit foreign interior, a café, saturated with the glamourous scent of dark coffee and aniseed-flavoured cigarette smoke from groups of men, deep in loud unintelligible conversation. Simultaneously a remembered song emerges like forgotten perfume from some ancient part of her brain; it leaks ephemeral snatches of jaded yearning about love and loss.

Then out of nowhere, comes a bizarre and chilling thought. She tries to tamp it down, but insidiously, it rises again. What if…what if a man with a gun were to come into the indoor pool and begin to shoot people? Ridiculous! She is no stranger to random, disturbing thoughts; sometimes quite ordinary things can trigger darkly potent images, but even though there has been a recent spate of lone killers and their inevitable carnage, she knows this is something else. It begins again, a vision in forensically clear detail. What if…she hears shooting, and in the time it takes for her to identify the sound, there are bodies, curved and bloodied fish, floating just beyond the spattered glass? What would she do, where could she go?

Surveying her options from the water, she realises how vulnerable she is; there is almost nowhere to hide, except possibly under the pool-cover that hangs from a giant spool in front of the fence, but it is so thin it offers little protection. And in the seconds before the gun man bursts upon her, what then? She could duck under the water, but the underwater lights are due on any minute and she can't take the risk. That leaves the fence with its hideous vertical slats. Would she really be able to scrabble, half naked and wet, up and over a six-foot fence and get back down the other side? She can almost feel the searing burn of a glancing bullet and, on her arm, the trace of its bloody furrow.

In panic, she tears madly across the carpark in the wet, screaming for help, her bare feet sliding on the muddy grass verge, and just beyond comes face to face with the prurient curiosity of staring shoppers who, struggling with loaded trolleys, instinctively swerve away from her.

That's enough, just stop it - this is getting out of hand…but as the voice of reason tries to stamp out this nonsense, a small but insistent wail from somewhere deep in her mid-brain, keeps repeating, 'But what if? WHAT IF…?'

Double Take

Winnie strikes up, takes a slow drag, slips into the reception area, gives her details to the sergeant on duty, and finds a spot on a bench. The place heaves with gloom. Townspeople haggard with worry stand in clusters. An officer calls, 'Winnifred Brogan' and calls again before she realises it's her own name. He points to a set of double doors.

Smillie had been polite enough with his request that day. After fawning over one of his clients, he'd cleared his throat. 'Mrs Brogan, err… Winnie, do you undertake any house-cleaning work, in addition to office caretaking?'

Winnie had folded her duster in half, folded it again and then once more, achieving that neatness she liked. He rarely spoke to her directly; she was invisible in her overalls. That suited her; she had no time for this man with his slicked back hair and stained teeth.

She stepped back and to the side. 'Aye, from time to time. Just for a bit of pocket money. It'll have to be early mornings.' It had to be while the girls were at school, and Joe was at the yard, so he'd be none the wiser about the extra cash coming in.

'Indeed.' Smillie swayed on the balls of his feet.

She put him out of his misery. 'I'll start on Monday, nine o'clock then, a trial you understand?'

'Very good of you.'

'It'll be ten shillings.' That was half again her usual rate.

'Perfectly reasonable. Thank you. It'll be some relief… It's Hill Road, Glenorchy House.' He'd muttered on, backing away like she was the bloody Queen of England.

Winnie thumbs out her ciggie and follows the officer to a

167

waiting room with rows of brass studded chairs. He leaves her alone, and she lumbers to the middle but, feeling hemmed in, bum-slides over the chairs to the end of a row, her dress shimmying up past her knees. She yanks it down.

On that Monday, she'd dressed plain for work. She'd come off the bus at the Municipal Rose Garden. It was splashed with reds, oranges and pinks, and she'd smiled at the little cherub projecting water from his ding-a-ling. She climbed the stairs set into the brae, careful of the crumbling stone flags, and turned into a tree-lined, well-heeled world. It was a grim morning, the rain coming at her in panels, but she was watertight in her rosebud Rainmate and flat patent boots. She read each name on the big gates until she finally reached Glenorchy House. Crunching up the drive, she was surprised to see Smillie's grey saloon parked in front of the garage. Winnie hadn't expected to see him. She thought his wife would be at home alone. He was always on to the clients about his good lady wife this and his good lady wife that.

The building was a dismal affair, cracks spidering across the front and grass spouting from the gutters. Giant rhododendron bushes, glowering without their flowers, dripped with rain. She pressed the nub of a brass buzzer and chimes rose far inside. The door creaked open, and Smillie appeared in a diamond-check dressing gown, feet poked into leather slippers, his spindly legs bare.

'I didn't expect to see you, Mister Smillie.' She glanced past him into the gloom of the hallway.

The tramlines in his face deepened. 'Ah, Winnie, my dear, so… grateful, err… you could come.'

He didn't move to let her pass quite quickly enough, forcing her to breathe in as she skimmed by.

'Where's Mrs Smillie?' Winnie hung her coat on the stand.

'Regret she's gone to her mother's in Edinburgh.'

Other side of the country, wouldn't be back anytime soon.

His eyes twisted down and she caught the reek of whisky.

'Where's the scullery?' she asked.

He stared at her as though she'd asked for a hundred pounds and flapped his hand towards a door at the back of the hall. The eejit had nothing to say for himself, but she was ready if he tried any cheek.

It was a big room, dank and dirty with one poky window streaming with rain, the paint around the panes peeling. She made a beeline for the cupboard door where a mop head leaned out dispiritedly. The wind keened outside, rain battered at the window, and water rushed down an eave's pipe, splashing onto the paving with a series of desolate splats. As the kitchen darkened, Winnie shivered and fumbled at a grimy switch. The room stuttered alight as she wiped her fingers on her pinny. It was like the rain was on her skin and in her bones, but this was work and ten bob was ten bob.

She filled the pail and shook in some Vim from the cupboard under the sink. The floor was covered in filthy rubber tiles, the sink was rimmed with yellow grease and the dirty pots on the cooker would have to be scrubbed hard.

Sniffing with distaste, she continued with her chores, quite forgetting about Smillie until, bent over the sink, her ears filled with the rush of tap water, she felt the weight of a hand on the rise of her bottom. The smell of whisky choked her; his breath was at her ear. She drove her elbow into his ribs. He groaned and, as she turned to face him, fell backwards onto the table, scattering chairs.

Winnie inched away from the sink. His eyes were full of accusation as he pulled himself to his knees. She knew that look and where it could end. It was Joe in his cups.

Her arm swung wildly behind her; her fingers clutched at a handle. The drawer stuck on its runners; she jerked it further. It came away, scattering metal to the floor. Too far to reach. Her body tightened, the last ladle settled, the vibrations ceased, the air filled with the sound of the old clock in the hall: tick, tick, tick… Smillie was on his feet, groping towards her, his fingers trembling, white spindly thighs visible as his dressing

169

gown slanted open. She skidded to the right and caught hold of a heavy pot. Its edge dunked skull; he grunted once and slumped to one knee, eyes bulging.

She ran; the drone of his choked laughter following her all the way to the front door, down the hill, and past the rose garden with its little cherub spilling water from his ding-a-ling.

In the waiting room, Winnie stares at the pattern on the tiles. Creamy, veined with orange, like real marble. She rubs it with her heel. Hard, no joins. Must be marble. Feels like it, looks like it, but looks can be deceiving. Actions can be deceiving too. And now she's here to explain her own. How's she going to do that? Except to say she might have been mistaken. How she wished she'd taken a moment to listen to the man. When she replays that morning, she can't be sure of events.

Maybe he'd touched her at just the wrong moment as she bent down, and she'd overreacted. Maybe the look in his eyes was desperation, not anger. Maybe he'd trousers on under the dressing gown.

Maybe she should've taken that one beat of the heart to consider things. She could've turned and said, 'Can I help you, Mr Smillie?'

In one beat, life would've gone on as before. In one beat, she wouldn't be sitting in this waiting room. In one beat, Mr Smillie wouldn't be lying on a mortuary slab.

She could've sat him down on a chair at the table and filled the kettle. 'A wee cup of tea, Mr Smillie?'

The waiting room dissolves around her, and she's back in that dreary kitchen, taking out two odd cups, one with rosebuds and the other yellow with a gold rim, and some sugar. The sugar has brown splotches and is hardened like cement, so she has to dig in the spoon to break it up. She finds a pot, a tea caddy and another spoon. There's a bottle of cold milk on the drainer. It must have been outside for a while; a bird's beak has punctured the foil.

The man sits with his head in his hands. Hands that are

gnarled, hands without a wedding band. No woman has been in this kitchen for at least a year.

She pours the scalding tea. Adds sugar and milk to his without enquiry. Has her own without the milk. Sits a decent way off but close enough to hear him. He looks up. Winnie's forced by proximity to meet his eyes. He seems a man demented. Despite the smell of whisky, he's sober. She knows enough about drinking men to know that, but still his fingers shake when lifting the teacup so that liquid spills onto the table. She leaves it, even though it grates to ignore such a mess.

He raises the cup to his mouth and slurps. The noise aggravates her. The tea seems to give him back some control. His hand's steadier when he puts down the cup. 'Sorry, I've made a mess...'

'Not at all. It's your own house.'

'Forgive me... a mess... I forgot you were coming this morning.'

Winnie nods, takes a sip of tea, glad of its warmth.

He falls silent again, staring at the floor, his breath catching from time to time. Winnie waits. She's patient, not her usual busy self. The leak outside the window grows louder as if to invade the room. Smillie doesn't notice, he's encased in misery, chin at his chest.

She could go or she could stay. She could call a doctor. But if she did, what would she say? Mr Smillie's not himself, he's had a good drink last night, the wife's gone, the place is a mess, and he's in a right odd mood. Hardly an emergency. Bugger it, she'd have to sort this out herself. She does, with the skill of a psychiatrist. She listens to his story. The man has money troubles and is over his head in certain 'business transactions'. His wife has filed for divorce.

Only one beat of the heart, and she wouldn't be sitting in the police station, the tick of the waiting room clock forcing her back to real time. It ticks louder and louder as she listens. Her jacket's too heavy, making her sweat. She wriggles out of it, settles it on the next seat and smooths it flat. She looks down at her fingers. No rings. It's strange how one bad decision can make you face up to your other choices. If she'd known what Joe was like underneath, she'd have run a mile, but she'd been far too young to see him for what he was. A man with a mean streak the length of a washing line.

In the end, men were just not worth the unwrapping.

In the end, she could only swear to what she remembered.

The waiting room tilts as footsteps in the hall tap towards the double doors. It's time. She holds her breath, stares at the door…

The double doors squeak. She gets up, her dress sticking to the warm seat. She pulls the fabric smooth.

'The Inspector will see you now. You all right, ma'am?' He has warm blue eyes and a face crisscrossed with age.

'Just a bit nervous.'

Although she never saw James Smillie dead, every night she wakes up with the image of his dangling body, head at an angle, the silk dressing gown swinging gently as the rain drums on the garage roof.

'Come, my dear.' The officer holds her gaze. 'You'll be alright. Everyone who waits here feels the same way. It'll all be over soon.'

In Search of Puffins

Looking down, I watch the litter as it blows, weightless, along the pavement 'til it gets stuck in the gutter. Then I see Jem, head down, hurrying round a corner and out of sight. I like Jem. He has trouble reading, doesn't bother writing, but I know he can because I've seen him do it on walls. He creates amazing pictures in a splash of aerosol paint, like the paint was his breath come gasping out the can. He speaks through paint and arcs of colour. That's his language.

From this walkway, I can see Dez's cafe, soot-ridden and boarded up. 'S been like that a while now, ever since it was torched. I look at my arms, my pale brown skin. Not black, not white, but a rich golden brown in-between. And I have my father's green eyes, bright like stars, my mum says. She tells me not to worry. But I do.

Now I see a dot of pink, holding hands with an even smaller dot of blue. That's gotta be Charlotte and her brother Aiden. Once her mum sent them out to the minimart to get bread, and Charlotte didn't let go of Aiden's hand all the way there and all the way back. Then they went home, and I didn't see them again for weeks. Perhaps they're out getting bread again. I watch them, and they go the same way Jem went and are gone. For a horrible moment I think they won't ever come back. I don't know why I think that. I rub my arms. I'm cold.

'Isha?'

Mum's the only one in our family who uses my name. My brother Tre doesn't. He never says 'Hey Isha, wanna hang out?' He's quiet and doesn't say much.

'Isha! Come in now. Your tea's ready.' I don't want to go in. I don't want tea. I look down again from the walkway hoping to see Charlotte and Aiden again, but I don't.

Inside the flat, Mum's sitting at the table, a plate in front of her. Looks like she's done chips and beans again.

How can I tell her I'm not hungry?

'Sure,' I say, and pull out a chair and sit with her.

She waits for me to start eating. I pick up a couple of hard dry chips and push them through the bean juice. She begins to eat as well. Little mouthfuls, chewed slowly, as though she's waiting for a tooth to fall out.

I take a deep breath because I've got something to tell her, but the door opens and Tre walks in; my deep breath doesn't go anywhere then, just stays inside me until I have to let it out slowly and hope that no-one hears.

'Your tea's under the plate,' Mum says to Tre, nodding to the worktop. Tre picks up his food and joins us at the table.

'It's cold,' he says, but eats it anyway.

'Are you going out later?' Mum asks.

'You eating that?' he says to me and tries to take my food.

'Hey!' I shout and move my plate out of his reach, which is stupid because I know I don't want the food, but I don't want him to have it either.

'Whatever,' he says. Then he goes, leaving his empty plate on the table, his chair sticking out in the middle of the tiny room like inconvenient roadworks.

'Mum,' I start to say, but she's not listening. 'Mum,' I say again a bit louder, and she looks at me. 'Miss Cole says I'm clever enough to go to Underhill.'

My words fill the air around us like a brewing thunderstorm.

'Miss Cole said I could pass the entry exam real easy.'

Slowly Mum puts her fork down.

'And why does Miss Cole think that?' she finally says, like she was accusing me of something.

'I'm not lying!' I blurt out. 'Miss Cole thinks I could do it.'

I wait for her to speak, my voice echoing in my head like I'm shouting at myself.

'You ain't going to no Underhill,' she says quietly.

I feel the rage burning through me then, right up through

174

me until it sticks in my throat and begins to hurt.

'Mum! Underhill! A proper school!'

I'm not like Tre - I love reading and writing and maths and science and my love for those things is a secret trying to escape like a lion from a cage. We sit in angry silence.

'Eat your tea,' Mum says, but I can't. I can't swallow anything. It hurts too much.

Me and Jem walk through the underpass on our way to school, and I can smell fresh paint. Casually he slows by a new piece. A large face with an orange beak, open wide like a lobster claw, peers at me from the side of the tunnel. Its bright little eye pierces the gloom.

'It's shouting,' he says.

'Birds don't shout,' I say.

'Yeah they do.'

'No, they don't,' I say.

I study it. It's just three colours: black, white and orange, but Jem's made it look like every colour is somewhere in the bird's face, like all the gases in the galaxy have met right here and exploded onto the wall.

'Puffin, right?'

'Yeah,' replies Jem, looking up and down the underpass as if he's keeping watch. 'Saw one in a book,' he says. 'C'mon.' We move away, along the underpass and into the daylight. I imagined us as puffins, coming out of our burrows and onto a carpet of grassland on a sandy cliff.

'I got a chance to go to Underhill.' Jem stops walking.

'That posh school?'

'Yeah.'

'You gonna go?'

'My mum won't let me. Says I got to go where everyone else goes.' Jem hitches up his bag, and I hear the soft rattle of the spray cans.

'I ain't ever going to school again. I'm just gonna bomb.'

'What, like Banksy you mean?' I laugh, imagining Jem throwing up his pieces of art all over the estate, covering every dirty wall and broken doorway with pictures of puffins and hawks and kestrels.

'I'm the new Banksy.'

'Jemsy,' I tease, but immediately see I've upset him. He looks to the ground, pulls on the straps of his bag again and starts walking away.

'Jem! Wait!'

I catch up with him, but his mood has changed, and he doesn't want to talk anymore. 'I'm sorry.'

'Go to Underhill,' Jem says flatly, then turns off down a road and walks away.

I run through the underpass, past Jem's puffin and out the other side where I slow down and catch my breath. I'm desperate to go home but don't want to go home at all. Miss Cole told me that my mum had phoned the school about Underhill and that me and her needed to talk.

But rounding the corner there's Jem with some bigger kids. I recognise one of them. It's Stephen Mansell - Manse to his crew - and Jem looks scared. His cans are scattered around, and he's pushed back against the wall. Manse kicks Jem's bag but Jem doesn't move.

Manse drags Jem away from the wall and shakes him hard, slaps him, then throws him to the ground. I want to go and help but I can't - I'm so scared. Jem doesn't move. I watch Manse push Jem's arm with his foot. Then he lifts Jem's whole arm and flips it, but it comes to rest on the ground just above Jem's head and still Jem doesn't move. I hold my breath: I think Jem is dead.

Manse sees me. For a second we stare at each other then suddenly he shouts something and runs, followed by his crew. Then I start running toward Jem, and I see him getting up and by the time I get to him I'm crying.

Jem slowly sets about picking up his cans and stuffing them back in his bag, and I grab one as I reach him.

'You ok?' I ask, holding out the can. I want to hug him, to make sure he's alright. 'Yeah,' he says. But I don't think he is.

'Why are you crying?'

'Thought you were dead,' I say. 'I thought...' but I couldn't say any more, and just hand him the can. He takes it, looking over his shoulder to double-check that Manse has really gone.

'C'mon,' he says, and we hurry away as fast as we can.

'My place?' I suggest. Jem used to come round a lot a few years ago, but then he just stopped. Started tagging instead. He went from random tagging to proper pictures almost overnight. It was like he'd swapped his bedroom for a life on the streets where he was free to paint what he wanted whenever he wanted.

As we get near my flat, I see Jem is limping.

'What did he want?' I ask. Jem gives a small shrug.

'Dunno,' is all he says. We get to the stairwell and Jem pauses.

'What?' I say to him, even though I know what he's thinking.

'I'm fine now.' And before I can say anything else, he turns round and heads the other way.

As I climb the steps home, I wonder what Miss Cole said. I get to our landing and walk slowly along the dead straight walkway, like I'm on the edge of a concrete cliff. I get to our door and push my key in the lock and feel hot and cold and sick all at the same time.

I open the door and Tre's already home. He stares at me.

'Alright?' he asks, and I'm so surprised I just stare at him.

'Is that you Isha?' Mum calls. I come in, but still Tre stands in front of me.

'You ok?' he asks me again.

'Yeah it's Isha,' he calls to Mum when I don't answer, so I push past him and go to the living room. Mum looks like she's been waiting for me, and I want to shout at her, but I can't so just stare at the floor instead.

'I spoke to Miss Cole today,' she said. I could feel my stomach churning and wanted to be out, like Jem, out on the street and far away. I drop into a chair sideways, leaving my legs dangling over the arm.

'Sit round properly,' Mum insists, and I raise my eyes to the ceiling. She has no idea. There are worse things in the world than sitting sideways in a chair. Reluctantly I move my legs.

'We talked about Underhill.'

'Yeah? So? Don't matter, does it? You said I couldn't go.'

'You going to Underhill?' Tre stood in the doorway staring at me like I'd been out all night.

'School reckons she could pass the exam to get into Underhill.' Mum turns her attention to Tre, and out of the corner of my eye I see him lean heavily on the doorframe.

'So, you going?' he asks.

No-one says anything.

'Mum?' I say.

Suddenly it sounds like there's a chance.

'Can I?'

When I find Jem a few days later he's scribbling in a sketchbook. He's sitting on a low wall that's covered in graffiti, down by the canal. I sit on the wall next to him and stare at the sludge-green water, empty cartons and cans floating on its surface like tiny bodies.

'Alright?' he says.

'My mum says I can try for Underhill,' I say.

'Cool,' he says quietly, and I know he's really happy for me.

We sit and watch the water for a while, then Jem passes me his sketchbook. He shows me the picture he was drawing. It's beautiful.

It's of a boat, sailing across a blue sea to an island. An island of puffins.

'That's me and you,' he says, pointing at two little figures at the front of the boat.

'We'll do that one day,' he says.

I study the picture and see the brightly coloured puffin beaks, scattered speckles of orange across the page.

'They're shouting,' I say.

'Yeah,' he says. 'They are.'

178

The Good Man

There was nothing to see in the village. The tiny cluster of lime-washed, slate-capped coastal dwellings had fallen asleep as the daylight drained away to the west in the late afternoon.

Nobody was about as the gale swept in unseen over the sea, throwing wild waves like prancing sea ponies hard against the shingle beach, gouging out deep troughs there and driving the stones ever closer to the road beyond.

On the edge of the village, washed in harsh yellow electric light, stood the huge bulk of the Antelope public house, its broad shoulders reminding the closest cottages of its immensity.

The talk at the bar was of the weather. Even the oldest fishermen could not remember a time when a winter storm had arrived so suddenly and with such ferocity. The forecast had been for a deepening low moving in from the Atlantic, but the speed of its advance had surprised everyone.

Sybil Louise sat alone in the cottage with a pot of tea left brewing on a tray by the fire. There were noises in the room. Sounds from the coals in the grate. Hisses, splutters and sharp cracks that demanded her attention.

Gradually she became aware of another noise, music in a different key, emanating from the mantle clock standing like some solid, ostentatious obelisk above the fireplace. She had never really noticed the sound, although it had always been there, tracking their marriage, its dependability simply taken for granted, like drawing breath.

She wished that John was here. How many times had she wished for that over the years? But she had known what to expect when she accepted him. The sea would always be his wife, his true love, and she a mistress.

But that was how it was for the girls who married fishermen. She would join the other women standing on the shingle endlessly gutting fish, layering herrings, cod and whatever else the boats supplied, into the boxes of ice until, worn out by drudgery, she would slip away, unnoticed by most, into death.

She wished that John was here. Today was their wedding anniversary. Her memories of the early years were vivid, and she drew on them, on nights like these, when she felt abandoned and needed the comforting warmth of the remembrance of a time when she was beautiful and desired.

The mantle clock had been a wedding present from John's parents. An ornate monstrosity that was unfashionable even then. She had been grateful for it initially, but now she kept it wound simply out of respect for them.

John had wanted children - they both had – but no little ones had arrived, despite their strenuous efforts at conception. But she had found contentment in her belief that she had married a good man.

She wished that John had not gone out this morning. But there could be no telling him. Once set on his course, there would be no halting or turning him. He would be rowing out to the fishing grounds to long-line for cod.

Sybil Louise put down the thick woollen sea jersey she had been darning and poured her tea. She locked her fingers around a willow patterned cup, remembering when she had bought the set in the market. Waste of money John had said gruffly when she thought that he would have been pleased. She did not intend drinking from a selection of chipped, unrelated china for the rest of their marriage she had told him. Waste of money he had reiterated, although he altered his opinion later that evening as they lay together, for she knew how to control her man. Beautiful it was, he acknowledged then, talk of the village we will be he had said and congratulated himself on having gained such a thoughtful and sophisticated wife. She had blushed with pride in the dark. The memory of it made her smile even now.

The clock chimed the hour. It was late and John was still not home. She guessed that the storm had overtaken him quickly. Rather than risk his life in a desperate race for home, Sybil Louise knew that he would have made for the nearest sheltered place. Someone on the coast would have given him a meal and a bed for the night – as would she in similar circumstances. For this was how it always had been in their community, where the sense of belonging was strong.

She drained her cup, placed it back on the tray and returned it to the kitchen. There were her best shoes, cleaned and buffed to star brightness, standing on newspaper laid on the floor. Beside them stood John's Sunday best boots, ready for church tomorrow. The church had always been important to them. They had been baptised and married there, as had their neighbours, and those who had run their mortal race now lay in the churchyard, a memory to those who had loved them in life.

Had John remembered their anniversary? Most years she wrote it on the calendar for him to discover. He had always taken her for a port and lemon at the Antelope in the evening, to celebrate. She smiled. Such a thoughtful man, a good man. She was lucky to have him.

It was cold in the bed despite the extra warmth of John's old army greatcoat that she had laid over it. She snuggled down, assumed a foetal position and attempted to warm a woman-sized area. How she wished John was with her. He knew how to warm her. She ran her hands gently over her inner thighs and thought of him, but it was no good. She was physically too cold to sustain an interest.

Outside, the gale continued tearing at the cottage walls like a demented, living thing, and out at sea the mountainous waves chased each other to shore where they fell onto the shingle beach, battering it mercilessly.

Sybil Louise wondered about John. Was he safe? Was he thinking of her right now, as she was of him? She knew his strength, both physical and mental, and he had been caught in unpredictable storms before.

But where was he?

It was the not knowing that she found so unsettling. Had he struggled ashore and knocked on the door of strangers, as his father had? He had knocked on a strange door once and had married the girl who lived behind it. That woman was John's mother.

Her pulse quickened. What if John had also found a woman, a willing woman, behind a cottage door and decided to stay forever? What then? A sudden panic gripped her. She could never sleep now and never would until her precious John was safely home to hold her in his strong embrace.

As the first silver strips of dawn shone out from under the solid slabs of night cloud, she stood at the kitchen sink splashing ice-cold water against her face in shallow handfuls, until the shock of it brought her back to full wakefulness. She carefully raked over last night's embers in the grate and, finding fire still present, fed it fuel until the flames caressed the flue like the tongues of angry dragons, and the familiar crackling sound began again.

She prepared breakfast, for John would be home soon and hungry. She filled the kettle, laid the oilcloth on the kitchen table and set her blue and white on it.

It would not be long. By now he would be pulling across the bay towards her, leaning back heavily on the oars with the inherited strength of generations.

Quickly she dressed, deciding that today, the day after their wedding anniversary, she would make herself look special for him, a reminder that she was his woman and ready for his taking if he needed her.

She ran a thin smear of red lipstick across her lips. John had found it in the bottom of the boat he said. Brand new it was. It must have belonged to one of the sight-seeing holidaymakers he sometimes ferried along the coast. No sense in wasting it, he said. And she remembered how he liked to see her wearing it.

The ornate hands on the ugly mantle clock slowly followed

each other round. It was mid-morning. John should have been home by now. She wondered if he had gone straight back to the fishing grounds, but the sea had not lost its wildness. The boats were still hauled up and held firmly to the beach by heavy iron. There would be no fishing today.

Poor John! How she would hold him! How she would smother his neck with kisses!

There was a loud knock on her door, a solid knock, a man's knock. Sybil Louise wrung her hands clean in her apron and stumbled on the flags as she raced for the door. It was John! She knew it was him. The silly man was knocking on his own front door when he knew it would be unlocked, and she would be waiting behind it. Tears of relief involuntarily flooded her eyes as she quickly checked her appearance in the hall mirror. She gripped the brass knob and wrenched the door open.

It was after one o'clock when both the policewoman and the coastguard left her alone with her tears and tea. John's body had been discovered, first thing that morning, floating face down in the calm water of a sheltered cove. His boat was found further out. He appeared to have been washed overboard and, unable to get back to the boat, had drowned.

Sybil Louise was numb with shock. Later she would howl with pain.

The coastguard had placed a large bunch of cellophane wrapped red roses on the table. Totally ruined by the sea water, they were now a sorry, soggy mess of velvet red petals and dark, kelp-coloured leaves that had been found slopping about in the boat. She looked forlornly at them lying in their decomposing wrapping, their sad, drooping heads reverentially bowed, perfectly in tune with the occasion. But now she knew for sure that, for the first time, John had remembered their wedding anniversary. This time he had not forgotten their special day. He had bought her roses!

There was the edge of a salt-stained card poking from between the ruined, gluey stems. She reached for it smoothing out the greasy cellophane with a finger. She could not see its entirety, but it was clearly a printed florist's card. She pushed further into the disintegrating mess and tugged it free, anxious to read John's words printed there in beautiful solid black ink. Their sentiment boldly stated, their intimacy indisputable, Sybil Louise read each one out loud:

FOR MY BEAUTIFUL REBECCA
WITH ALL MY LOVE AS ALWAYS
YOURS
JOHN
X

Parlez-Moi D'Amour

'It was the most frightful storm,' Dolly Baignton told me. 'It woke me up in the early hours. I thought the roof tiles were being torn off. The noise was extraordinary, but through it all I could hear the piano downstairs. Dear MT was playing so wildly, it's surprising she didn't break the strings.'

She was talking of Emmeline Thornbury, who was to become Dame Emmeline in due course thanks, not least, to her series of Weather Paeans, that remarkable series of concerti that cemented her place forever in the walls of the hall of fame of music.

'How can I describe it? The howls, the sighs, the groans. Like a herd of banshees—is that the right word? A herd? They were certainly heard not seen. It's all there in the music, you know. You have heard the piece, haven't you, young man?'

I hadn't been called young for decades, but then Dolly was over ninety and had the right. The occasion she described was a holiday she and Emmeline had taken in 1926, in a remote cottage on Exmoor. Emmeline had just received a commission through Leslie Boosey, the music publisher from the Hammersmith Philharmonic Society for, he said, 'a concerto for bandoneon and strings, my dear, whatever a bandoneon is'. I asked old Fuller-Maitland, and he said it was some form of South American squeezebox. They're entertaining some visiting virtuoso. Still, de gustibus non est disputandum, my dear, and they are offering £40.' [I looked the phrase up later – there is no disputing about tastes. Beyond my schoolboy Latin, I'm afraid, which I failed ignominiously.] Since they wished the concerto written in a mere three weeks, Emmeline had sought the seclusion of Exmoor to work uninterrupted on the piece.

When they arrived, Emmeline was delighted to find the

cottage had an old piano in the parlour. She immediately sat down and started hammering out the popular song *Parlez-moi d'amour*, which was all the rage in Paris at the time, improvising variations on it while Dolly cooked supper. The next day was set fair, and Emmeline went out for a ramble "to clear my head, Dolly". She returned in the late afternoon in high dudgeon. No inspiration had come to her. All evening she stomped around, occasionally stopping at the piano to thump out *Parlez-moi d'amour* again. That night the storm broke, and Dolly woke to hear the howling wind. Emmeline was not in bed and must have risen for some reason. Then through the noise of the storm, Dolly heard the sound of the piano below. Emmeline was composing. She had found her stimulus in the wild weather.

After that, Emmeline worked like a demon. Dolly told me of her days:

'MT was possessed. She would go out for tramps at any hour, returning to murder the piano. I feared she would break it, but it was a sturdy little workhorse. I tiptoed around making sure she ate and drank and changed her clothes. She didn't seem to notice what she ate, even though I took a lot of trouble over our meals. It was a tense time. Sometimes I took the Morris Oxford and drove into Minehead for provisions. I remember one time I took tea in a café. The waiter was charming and very attentive; I felt positively flattered. MT would have been furious had she known. She hated anyone showing any interest in me. But it helped me through a trying period.'

She took a sip of her tea, nibbled a biscuit and looked a little wistful. I wondered how much her support had bolstered Emmeline in her work. As if reading my mind, she continued:

'One night, Emmeline came to bed very late. She said softly, which was not like her, "Dolly, I've been neglecting you. This thing is possessing me, but it's good, it's good. When it's out, I'll make it up to you." I felt proud of her.

'It was after about ten days, I suppose, when one afternoon

while I was making scones for tea, she flung the kitchen door open and stood there, like a cloud parting to reveal the sun. "It is done," she said. "I have finished, and it is splendid. They will have never heard anything like it." She crushed me in a hug of joy. "Find some champagne, Dolly, or wine or cooking sherry, whatever there is, and I will play it to you, and you will be amazed."

'She led the way to the piano and played through the concerto. I can't describe how she managed to convey the effect of bandoneon and strings on a simple piano, but she generated extraordinary noises, the bandoneon sighing and wheezing like the storm, the strings sliding and fluttering, and every now and then, fragments of *Parlez-moi d'amour* as if half-heard through the noise of the wind. Though I was not a trained musician, I knew that this was an important moment in her music.

'Afterwards, she was radiant, and I was so happy for her. We must have opened a second bottle of wine because the next thing I remember it was morning, and a man outside was shouting that he had a telegram.

'I went down and brought it back up to MT. I remember exactly what it said: "Hold fire my dear. Mandolin not bandoneon. Asses at Hammersmith confused. Boosey."'

'My God,' I said, 'that must have been an awful shock. How did she take it?'

'She was very still and quiet for a long time,' said Dolly. 'I didn't like to move for fear she might think I didn't care. Eventually she said, "Take me into Minehead, Dolly. I will telephone Boosey."

'We got up, and without stopping for breakfast or even a cup of tea, I drove her into town. At the Post Office, she telephoned London. I heard what she said. I think all of Minehead heard her. "You imbecile," she shouted, "of course I can't rewrite it for mandolin. A mandolin goes plinky-pluck, whereas a bandoneon goes waa-waa. You can't make roast beef from a Dover sole." That was a strange thing for her to say, for she could not even boil an egg.

'She was terrible company for the rest of the day. Moody, surly, silent, except when she muttered darkly under her breath. As though influenced by her, the skies turned dark and it began to rain, not hard but relentlessly. After supper, MT went outside. I could see her standing there in the dark, no raincoat or umbrella. I knew I must leave her on her own. She would be awfully angry with me if I interfered. So, I went up to bed, not expecting to sleep.

'I must have nodded off, however, because the next thing I knew she was shaking me. She was drenched but glowing. "Have you ever listened to the rain, Dolly? Dripping on this, on that, different rhythms, cross-rhythms? All you have to do is use your ears." She went out of the room. I heard her clunking downstairs, and then the piano started up. On and on, pounding.

'By next morning it was well under way—the new Mandolin Concerto. She had simply started all over again.

'And the result was we left Exmoor a week later with not one but two new pieces—the first two of the Weather Paeans, Storm and Rain. It was the beginning of a very exciting time, young man. A turning point in British music. Oh, she was a great woman!'

She picked up her tea again and smiled in recollection. The woman in the next chair leaned over to me and said in a dry whisper, 'It's the horses, you know.'

I thanked Dolly profusely and said goodbye. Outside the home, it was drizzling. Dame Emmeline Thornbury had not written a Paean called Drizzle. It was far too grey for her, I suppose.

The Authors

Anil Classen - Sento
Anil, born in South Africa, is a German writer of Indian descent living in Switzerland, with an academic background in Psychology, English and Journalism. Shortlisted for the *Spotlight First Novel Award*, his work has featured in *The Tulip Tree Review*.

Valerie Thompson - Mabel Mulvaney is Writing a Book
In no particular order: keen gardener, aspiring beekeeper, hopeful writer, feminist, ailurophile. This story is for everyone who longs to write a book, who longs to have written a book, but who can't get to grips with that pesky bit in-between.

Ed Walsh - On Cortez Street
Writer of novels and short stories. After finishing paid employment, I now dedicate more time to writing, not that that makes it any easier. I have no website or blog, having only recently accommodated the ball-point pen.

James Woolf - Mo
James' stories have been published widely in the UK. He also writes scripts for the theatre and his award nominated play, 'Empty in Angel', will be appearing at different venues when theatres reopen. You can read more about James on his website woolf.biz

Stephanie Percival - Verity and Justine
Stephanie enjoys writing in a variety of styles and genres. Her work has been long and shortlisted and has won several creative

writing competitions. She has published a novel, 'The Kim's Game' and a novella, 'The Matter' with *Cinnamon Press*. www.stephaniepercival.com

Martin Barker - Matchsticks and Zombies
Born on a funfair, the son of a travelling showman, I live in Poole, Dorset and have recently rediscovered my love of storytelling. I write flash fiction and short stories, and I am currently working on my first novel.

Christine Breede - Silent Home
Christine holds an MS from Columbia University, serves as a speech therapist for the International School of Geneva and organises writers' workshops. She was nominated for the *Pushcart Prize 2020* and is currently at work on her first novel.

Hannah Abigail Peters - Chaperone
Hannah writes long and short fiction alongside working for charities and non-profit groups. She has lived in London for 20 years but originally hails from Yorkshire. In her spare time, as well as writing, she enjoys working in her garden. She will publish another short story in a forthcoming *Inky Lab Press* anthology.

Elizabeth Jane Andreoli - The Goddess and the Fire Dancer
I love art and language. The short story brings them together, creating a mood and a verbal image in a tiny frame. Joining a storytelling club allowed me to express my ideas, with the discipline of a monthly deadline.

Joe Bedford - The Seagull
Joe is a writer from Doncaster, England. His short stories have been published widely, including in *Litro, Structo and Mechanics' Institute Review*, and are available to read at joebedford.co.uk. You can reach him via Twitter @joebedford_uk

Sam Szanto - Don't Refuse Me
Sam lives in Twickenham with her family. More than 20 of
her stories and poems have been published in print and
online, and listed in competitions. Sam won the *2020 Charroux
Poetry Prize* and the *First Writers International Poetry Prize*.

Karen Tobias-Green - The Snowman
Karen writes poetry, prose fiction and arts and culture
reviews. She teaches Creative Writing in an arts university and
runs sensory writing workshops. She has recently completed
her DPhil.

Conor Duggan - The Egg and the Skipping Rope
Conor is an Irish writer of short stories, Limerick poems and
prose. He previously studied and worked as a geologist, and he
is currently studying fiction in Norwich. He is a fan of comedy,
work play and puns.

Akhil Bansal - Through the Window
Akhil is a junior doctor and aspiring writer. He is passionate
about health education and equality, as well as foregrounding
voices that are often forgotten. This piece is about how young
adults in particular have struggled with the isolation of
COVID, based on the experience of Akhil and his friends.

Benjamin Peter Taylor - Cocoa Tea
Benjamin has had a love of reading and writing from an early
age. 'Cocoa Tea' is inspired by his appreciation of the people
of Dominica.

Emily Howes - Little Hell
Emily Howes lives in London. She loves storytelling in all its
forms and has written and directed for radio, theatre and
television. She is also currently studying for an MA in
Existential Psychotherapy. Her work can be viewed at
www.emilyhowesdirector.co.uk

Jan Halstead - Just Like Morse
Jan is an occasional writer of articles and short stories. Her stories have previously been published by the women's magazine market and in an HHA competition anthology, *Come into the House.*

Silvia Rucchin - Showgirls
Silvia is based in South London and is currently undertaking an MA in Creative Writing. Her writing, like the short-story piece *Showgirls*, is the product of – or reaction to – growing up in a hamlet of about thirty people.

Gerry Webber - Punch Drunk -
Gerry lives in Edinburgh where he is a member of the Stobie Stories writing group. He has published a number of short stories in *The Anti-Zine*, *Far Off Places* and in the *Iron Press 'Aliens'* collection (forthcoming 2021).

Penelope Anne Mapp - The Friend
After 40 years living and working in South Africa and Namibia, my husband and I returned to the UK in 2016 and retired to Kingsland, Herefordshire. In January 2020, I joined a creative writing group. 'The Friend' is my first competition attempt.

Jack Sutherland - Big Truth
Jack is a writer from New Zealand, currently based in the smoggy bustle of Seoul, South Korea. Having published stories in Korea, Ireland and the US, Jack takes great pleasure in fiction that traverses the absurd on its way to the poignant.

Beverley Byrne - Chives are Onions Too
Previously a lecturer in Film History, Beverley is a journalist specialising in travel, interiors and celebrity interviews for national magazines and newspapers. Trading fact for fiction,

a passion for adventure frequently inspires her short stories which are published in several anthologies.

Tabitha Bast - There is Life at this Level
Tabitha lives in Leeds and is a therapist and occasional writer. Latest hits include another pandemic story 'You Will Have Heard of the Vet of Wuhan', published by *Creative Futures*, and article 'The Boys are Alright' in *Dope Magazine*.

Simon Dawson - On the Road Again
Simon is the author of six bestselling books including 'Pigs in Clover' and 'The Boy Without Love'. Simon is a writer, radio presenter and self-sufficient smallholder living in North Devon. www.simon-dawson.com/

Jenny Tunstall - Another Pineapple
Jenny writes for pleasure and because not writing is not an option. She has previously been short-listed for the Canadian *CBC Annual Literary Awards* (2004) and she won the *Bridgwater Prize* in 2012.

Ali Said - Both at Once
Ali is a mixed-race, gay Londoner. His work has been listed for several prizes and his non-fiction story, 'Aiden Shaw's Penis', is the title piece of an anthology released in May 2021. Ali can be found on Twitter @AliSaidWrote.

Emily White - The Skirt
Emily was inspired to write by her late husband, the poet Brian Nisbet. Poetry, flash and short fiction are her genre, and she is studying creative writing at Oxford University's Department for Continuing Education. She is a professional musician, specialising in a type of trombone called the sackbut.

K.A. Bigelow - The Ice Cream Man
I have written more than a hundred short stories and was recently named a finalist for the Saturday Evening Post's *Great American Fiction Contest*. I have always believed and taught that story and humour are fundamental human traits (like hiccups)

Sarah Murray - The Welsh Hill Farm
Sarah was trained as a museum curator but became an English teacher in 2015 after nearly 20 years living on a hill farm in Wales. She combines teaching and writing, and loves walking in the countryside.

Vaughan Edmonds - The Girl Dancing the Tarantella
Vaughan is a writer from South London. 'The Girl Dancing the Tarantella' is the first short story Vaughan has submitted to a writing competition and is his first published work.

Ruth Geldard - What If?
Artist and writer Ruth Geldard has had exhibitions that include Royal Academy London, and she has written for many art publications. A Faber graduate shortlisted for the *Fish Prize* and a finalist for *The London Independent Story Prize*, she has work in various anthologies.

Maureen Cullen - Double Take
Maureen is a retired social worker and has an MA in Creative Writing from Lancaster University. She has been shortlisted in various writing competitions and has poems and short stories published in magazines and anthologies.

Jacci Gooding - In Search of Puffins
Jacci won *Writing Magazine's* horror story competition, was runner-up in *The Squat Pen Rests* short story competition and was shortlisted for *The Bedford International Writing Competition*. She completed Oxford University's Creative Writing Undergraduate Course and reviews for *The Short Story*.

Jan Steer - The Good Man
Published novelist, short story writer and poet with a creative writing MA, Jan lives in a remote part of West Wales. He draws inspiration for his work from the beautiful Welsh countryside and the people living in it.

Oliver Barton - Parlez-Moi D'Amour
Oliver used to write computer user manuals but, having retired, now prefers to replace telling facts that nobody reads with writing whimsical fiction that more people can enjoy. He lives in Abergavenny, Wales.

Printed in Great Britain
by Amazon

61075945R00119